"Sugar, you su...

"Yes, Travis, I'm sur...

Her words didn't spu... ...ment so she tried again. "We've got a perfectly good bed right here. And you know we've been heading in this direction for days."

"Weeks…months." He added his own highly exaggerated number to her assessment. "But…"

"Don't. I don't want to think of the reasons why not. Not now. It's been a very long time since I've been in a man's bed. I haven't wanted to. But in your case—I do."

"I admit we've got—a thing—going on between us. But it's just lust. You're a better person than that."

She noticed he'd said *she* was a better person. But he wasn't? He was weakening. Good.

"I've been through a lot today, Travis. I almost died. Let's both lose our heads. Just for tonight. What we do will never have to leave this room."

Dear Readers,

Texas Manhunt, the second book in my Chance, Texas series is about justice and guilt. Summer Wheeler needs justice for her lost baby and doesn't care what it takes to reach her goal. She comes to Chance, Texas, to find the man who participated in ruining her life and bring him to justice.

Rancher Travis Chance likes to control his world, but he's also on a life mission to help lost souls. When Summer arrives and needs his help, he has no idea where it will take him. Or how helping Summer will change his whole life.

Summer is just as surprised to find she still has the capacity to love. Travis and his seven-year-old daughter show her the way to find a new life—through love.

I loved writing about two people who seem so unsuited for each other. Travis is a different kind of hero for me. But I loved writing about a man who everyone seems to love and yet is hated so bitterly by a few.

While writing this book, I surprised myself with a few twists I hadn't seen coming. Hope you enjoy reading it as much as I enjoyed the writing.

Happy reading,

Linda

LINDA CONRAD

Texas Manhunt

ROMANTIC
SUSPENSE

PB F CON
1642 3629   4-25-12   LJB
Conrad, Linda L.

Texas manhunt

SDW

Recycli
for this
not exist

ISBN-13: 978-0-373-27775-9

TEXAS MANHUNT

This edition published by arrangement with Harlequin Books S.A.

For questions and comments about the quality of this book please contact us at Customer_eCare@Harlequin.ca.

www.Harlequin.com

Printed in U.S.A.

LINDA CONRAD

When asked about her favorite things, Linda Conrad lists a longtime love affair with her husband, her sweetheart of a dog named KiKi and a sunny afternoon with nothing to do but read a good book. Inspired by generations of storytellers in her family and pleased to have many happy readers' comments, Linda continues creating her own sensuous and suspenseful stories about compelling characters finding love.

A bestselling author of more than twenty-five books, Linda has received numerous industry awards, among them a National Readers' Choice Award, a Maggie, a Write Touch Readers' Award and an *RT Book Reviews* Reviewers' Choice Award. To contact Linda, to read more about her books or to sign up for her newsletter and/or contests, go to her website, www.lindaconrad.com.

With all my thanks to fantastic author, Internet guru and psychic extraordinary Melissa Alvarez for her invaluable help with the horse complications.
Any mistakes are my own.
And to my sister-in-law Suzy Sankpill, longtime owner and lover of Arabian horses; one day I'll write about Arabians, I promise.

Chapter 1

Dear God, please not now.

Despite her prayer, the engine's normal *chuga-chug* dissolved into a series of terrible, raspy noises. Puffs of black smoke began streaming from under the hood.

Looked like she might not make it after all, and less than a mile short of the town. Shrugging off the inevitable, Summer Wheeler chalked it up to just another obstacle in a life that had turned from pure gold to a handful of dirt.

She fought the wheel and tried to baby her car to the side of the road. Desperate to make the ancient Ford Escort roll just a little bit farther before the engine quit for good, she barely looked up as a pickup truck passed, heading in the opposite direction.

Out of the corner of her eye, she noted that both the cowboy driving and the one riding shotgun turned to stare at her, a stranger in a funny old Ford, as they slowed down to pass her by. The truck didn't stop, but they got a good look as they kept going.

For a second, what she was seeing didn't register. Then it did.

The man riding in the passenger seat was *him!* That last tip she'd gotten about finding him in this little town must've been correct after all. It was the man she'd been seeking. She would never in a million years forget that face. It had starred in her nightmares for too long.

Had he recognized her? She threw the car into park and jumped out just as her engine died. Turning to the receding truck, she squinted at its license but couldn't get a good look.

White pickup. Some kind of writing on the side. She hadn't even managed to catch the make of the truck.

He must live here. Or nearby. After all the dead ends and frustration, not to mention spending every last dime of her insurance money, for the first time in five years she had him in her sights.

That settled it. Chance, Texas, would be her temporary new home. At least until she found out where he lived and worked, so she could inform the local authorities.

Evil must meet justice. Her entire life revolved around finishing things where that man was concerned. And she wasn't sure she could stand to go on looking for him much longer.

Turning, she threw a disgusted glance over at her dead car and sighed. The Ford wasn't going any farther. Nothing to do now but walk into town.

She adjusted her small backpack over her shoulder and carefully locked her car to start out hiking. Long shadows loomed across the road, reminding her that a cool night-time would soon overtake the stifling heat of the south

Texas day. Late fall in this part of the country seemed ripe with changing weather.

She hoped the Welcome to Chance sign she'd just passed was right and the town was close by. She needed to make it there before dusk turned the skies pitch-black and she became stranded in the dark at the side of the road. But she'd driven for what had seemed like forever without seeing the first sign of civilization. That pickup was one of only two vehicles she'd seen in the last half hour.

If the town was really that close, where was everyone? She hoped Chance wasn't such a small town that it wouldn't have a gas station where she could take the car for repair.

Not that she could afford to fix her wreck of a car, even if there was a mechanic in the town. The Ford needed a complete overhaul. Badly. But considering she had only twenty-five bucks and change left to her name, doing anything about—or to—the car would have to wait.

Earning money would have to come first. Summer refused to consider the possibility that she wouldn't be able to find some kind of work in Chance, even if the town was tiny and remote. She didn't have a lot of job experience, but she wasn't afraid to get her hands dirty. Over the past few months she had taken jobs as a waitress and a dishwasher and a motel maid. Something would turn up here, too.

She was just lucky her money hadn't run out before now. This time… This town… Must be the end of her journey. The goal she had dreamed of, worked for, needed to be realized very soon.

But right now her first priority had to be the car and finding a place to stay for the night.

Looking up as shades of black and deep red streaked

over the sky, she took a deep breath, and smelled rain. A storm must be on the way. Great. Exactly what she needed.

She picked up her pace. The trees along the side of the road bent their branches against the onslaught of winds, and dust devils suddenly raked at their leaves with angry abandon. Wrapping her arms around her body, she began to shiver.

At the very moment when a few buildings in the distance began to take shape, a cannon roar of thunder broke through the afternoon silence. She started to jog.

As she neared the edge of town, the first object she could make out was a big barnlike structure with a huge sign proclaiming it to be the Feed and Seed store. Across the road from that was what she'd hoped to find. A shabby single-story structure that looked as if it could've been a livery stable at one time, but was now outfitted with a couple of gasoline pumps, a diesel pump and a mechanic's bay, which currently held the biggest, blackest SUV Summer had ever seen.

No signs appeared anywhere on the building at all. Not above the bay or even on what appeared to be an office. Summer prayed that didn't mean the station was a private concern. On the other hand, she didn't have any money and certainly no choice, so what real difference did it make?

An old man sat on a rickety-looking metal chair beside the front door of the office, an unlit pipe stuck in the corner of his mouth. He called out to someone unseen when he spotted her heading in his direction.

A man, probably in his fifties, came out from behind the SUV. Wiping his hands on his coveralls and studying her carefully through his eyeglasses, he walked in her direction. "Where'd you pop in from, young lady? Storm's coming. You lost?"

She didn't want to answer that question with the truth—that she had been searching for this place for the last five years.

So she said instead, "My car broke down." She twisted around and waved in the general direction of where she'd left the Ford. "Back about a half mile down the road. Good thing I was close."

"Outta gas? If you'll give me a few minutes to finish up here, I'll drive you out, with enough gas to bring your car back to the pump."

She shook her head. "I don't think it's only out of gas. The engine was making a terrible noise before it died. And I saw some nasty, black smoke coming from under the hood."

The mechanic frowned but turned to the old man. "Dad, take the tow and bring it in for her." He stopped to glance up at the menacing sky. "Maybe wait a bit and see how bad the storm turns first. What kind of car you got, lady?"

"It's a Ford. Escort. About fifteen years old."

The mechanic shook his head, then wiped off his hands on an oily towel and with a wide grin stuck out one giant paw. "Name's Jimmy Stockard. I own this place. Do all the work on cars around here."

Hesitating, she took his hand. "I'm Summer Wheeler. Nice to meet you. I hope my car is fixable. It seems pretty far gone." The handshake went as well as could be expected for a woman who loathed touching strangers, and the actual skin-to-skin moment was blessedly over in a hurry.

"I can fix anything." Jimmy stashed the rag in his waistband and studied her. "We don't work on many of the larger ranch vehicles, 'cause most the spreads 'round these parts have their own mechanic's shops on-site for that kind of work. But when it comes to trucks or cars, anything that runs on petroleum, I'm your man. We'll handle it for you. Come on inside before it starts pouring."

The first few drops hit her in the face as she and Jimmy made a dash for the office. The old man ambled in right behind them.

Summer turned her keys over to the old man. He refused to look at her directly but mumbled, "Ma'am."

She couldn't help but consider him with skepticism, as he limped to an old tow truck parked right under the garage's overhang.

"Don't worry," Jimmy said. "My dad's the best tow-truck driver in this part of the state. Your car will be on the lift and on its way to fixed as soon as the storm's over."

"Um…" She had better stop him before things went too far. "How much is this going to cost? I'm…ah…kind of short on funds at the moment. As a matter of fact, I'm not sure I can even pay for the tow."

Jimmy grinned again. "You have family or friends in Chance? Maybe they can help."

"No. I'm afraid I don't know anyone in town." At least, not anyone who would admit to knowing her.

It was Jimmy's turn to look skeptical. "We don't get many people just passing through. Chance is kinda out of the way. Where you headed?"

She was about to answer when another fellow appeared out of the shadows in the far side of the bay. A good-looking man of around thirty, he was dressed in Western garb but didn't seem to be a regular, working cowboy. His boots weren't scuffed, and they looked as if they'd probably cost him a bundle. And the clothes he wore—designer jeans, she thought—were expensively styled and worn low on his hips. In fact, the arrogant way he stood, tall and with an erect bearing, could lead someone to believe he actually owned the place.

Since the new man didn't speak, Summer answered Jimmy. "I wasn't really headed anywhere. I've been traveling around the state—sort of sightseeing. Wanting to learn the lay of the land. I'm considering moving to Texas permanently, and I guess I took a wrong ranch-to-market road and ended up turned around."

Jimmy was still smiling. "Easy enough to do, once you're off the interstate. Everything looks the same in this part of Texas."

He turned his head then and sent a deferential glance to the stranger. "I'll be with you in a second, Travis. Your SUV is all set. Just needs one last tweak, and you'll be ready to go."

"No rush, Jimmy."

Summer didn't want to seem rude by staring at the stranger, but he was rather flagrantly staring at her. If he could ogle, so could she. She took a moment to study his sharp, green eyes, which were at the moment scrutinizing her from head to toe. His broad shoulders. The proud chin.

He gave off the aura of a man with a strong presence. A man who ruled things with an iron will and few words.

When his eyes met hers and held, her pulse kicked up, pounding blood through her veins and almost leaving her breathless. Crazy. She hadn't noticed a man in that particular way for years. And not even her late husband had made her heart race with a single glance.

But this was not the time, and she didn't have the inclination, to pay attention to how her body reacted to any man. Only one man was on her current agenda. But first she had to find him.

Summer calmed her thudding heart. Was this another

of the signs the doctors had warned might trigger a re-currence of her traumas?

Blinking, she told herself she was only having a normal reaction to an overpowering male. No one here was threat-ening her. And she was clearly not retreating to the fan-tasy world she'd occupied for months and months, even while the worst of her real world had spun around her.

Everything here was all too real.

Jimmy cleared his throat to catch her attention, and she dragged her gaze back to him. "Look," he began. "As soon as the storm lets up we'll tow you in and give the engine a look-see. We can talk about price and payments then. I know we'll come to some arrangement."

She nodded, not sure what to say to that.

"But it's late," he went on. "You're going to need some-place to stay—at least for tonight."

"Is there a motel in town?"

The stranger stepped forward and gave Jimmy a nod. "Excuse me, Ms. Wheeler," he interrupted. "I couldn't help overhearing. I'm Travis Chance. I run the Bar-C Ranch and have lived in this town all my life. Afraid there aren't any motels."

He wasn't done talking, but she broke in. "Your last name is Chance? Like the town? Did they name it after you?"

"The first of my ancestors to settle around here named the ranch and the county, along with the town he built, after himself. Would've named the whole state Chance, too, but he was a little late for that. Yessir, Ezra Chance wasn't a particularly modest man, but then, most Texans of his time would've done the same thing."

She noted a twinkle in this Chance's sober eyes, though his mouth never cracked a smile. Interesting.

"I think you'll find Chance is a fairly friendly place,"

Travis went on. "We'll locate someone to take you in for the night. Are you hungry?"

"Um..." She hadn't thought about food in so long she drew a blank. "I suppose so. Is there a restaurant in Chance?"

Without answering, Travis turned his head to speak to Jimmy. "Lend us your pickup, and we'll go over to Macy's for a bite to eat and have ourselves a little chat. Meanwhile, you finish up with the SUV and tow her car in. After supper I'll call Reverend and Mrs. Pike. They'll surely make room for her.

"We'll be back..." He continued speaking to Jimmy as he reached for her hand "...in about an hour or two to collect the SUV and her things from the Ford. Okay?"

Travis didn't seem too concerned whether or not his arrangements were all right with her and Jimmy. He didn't wait for an answer and just dragged her away. She wasn't crazy about having her hand held by a near-stranger's, but he didn't give her a chance to complain.

"You'll like Macy's food," he told her as he strode toward an old blue pickup at the side of the bay. "It's the only eating place in town, but she does a terrific Texas barbecue plate. I think we can beat the worst of the storm there if we hurry."

As though to agree, her stomach rumbled at the word barbecue. Travis didn't appear to notice. He was intent on shoving her up into the passenger seat of the old pickup.

Well, she was hungry. And if he turned out to be a serial killer, she wouldn't lose too much. She hadn't had anything to lose for a long, long time. If this was the night she was destined to die, Texas barbecue sounded like a great last meal.

Travis Chance chided himself for once again stepping into someone else's business. And another lost soul, at that. He'd given his word to Aunt June just last Sunday that he would stop picking up strays and giving money to people who would only drink it down or shoot it up. Looked like he would never learn.

But this young woman seemed different. There was something about her that drew him.

Yeah, yeah. She had the sexiest eyes he'd seen in longer than he could remember. Big, wide, and a shade of iridescent-blue he couldn't put a name to.

But that had nothing to do with giving someone a hand and being hospitable. Mostly, he was trying to do a good deed—and he was curious about her.

At about five foot eight, she stood slender and slightly bent, like a sapling against the wind. There was something fragile in the way she held her head. As though at any moment she would be struck down by an invisible hand.

He had to find out more about her. And seeing that she got a good, hot meal in the meantime would set his mind at ease.

They made it to Macy's Café just as the heavens opened up. He parked and raced around the pickup to the passenger side, trying to help her down without getting wet. But when he got there, she'd already climbed out and was moving toward the door at a good pace.

As he slipped inside the café right behind her, he came to the conclusion she might have a stronger center than he'd first thought. His curiosity burned brighter.

Macy's place was nearly empty. A couple of hands appeared to be finishing their suppers at one table, while old Mrs. Murphy sat alone at the counter. All of them turned to look as he found a table and showed Summer to a seat.

"Evening, Travis." Mrs. Murphy swiveled around on her barstool to give him a bright smile. "Not such a pleasant night, I'm afraid. You should be home eating one of Rosie's suppers, instead of out in this storm."

"Yes, ma'am." Travis removed his Stetson and placed it on an empty chair. "Except Rosie's off for a few days to San Antonio on a trousseau-buying trip."

Mrs. Murphy cast a blatant and curious glance at Summer. "I see. What about Jenna?"

The third degree. Wasn't that just typical of half the nosy population of Chance?

"Jenna's been staying in town with her great aunt this week. I intend to pick her up on my way out to the ranch."

By this point, Mrs. Murphy wasn't paying a bit of attention to his words. Her sole focus centered on Summer. Heaven forbid a new person should come to town without her being introduced.

Shaking his head, Travis gave in and gestured to the young woman at his left. "Mrs. Murphy, this is Summer Wheeler. Her car broke down up the road, and Jimmy will be towing it in to check it out when the storm lets up."

The temptation proved too much for the old lady. She climbed down from the stool and came over to stand next to the table, instead of shouting across the room. He didn't have a choice. Pushing his chair back, he stood.

"How do you do, young lady?" Mrs. Murphy said as she gazed down at Summer. "Do you have relatives in town? Can't say I recognize the name Wheeler from around Chance."

Summer, still fiddling with her silverware and napkin, kept her seat and didn't seem inclined to shake hands. But Mrs. Murphy didn't seem interested in shaking, either.

Still holding the fork in her right hand, Summer glanced up at the older woman. "I don't know anyone here, I'm afraid. I was lost when my car broke down. But Chance seems like a nice place." She nodded her head toward him. "Mr. Chance here was kind enough to offer me a ride to the café for dinner."

Mrs. Murphy beamed down at her. "Ah, yes. That's our Travis." She threw him an indulgent look. "Takes an interest in everyone in town. But, well, I suppose he should. He and his family do own most everything for miles around."

Travis squirmed in his boots, not sure what to say. Mrs. Murphy opened her mouth as though she had another question for Summer. But luckily, Macy, the owner of the café, barged out of the kitchen right then, her hands full of steaming plates.

"Hi, Travis. Be right with you." Macy set a couple of plates down on the counter. "Come get this food 'fore it gets cold, Aunt Betty." Then without waiting for a reply, Macy spun, heading off in the direction of the other occupied table.

After Mrs. Murphy mumbled something about it being nice to meet Summer and headed back to her seat, Travis let out a breath he hadn't known he was holding, and sat back down. The old lady's stool was too far away for her to eavesdrop, if he kept his voice down.

"Do you really own everything for miles around?" Summer's eyes were wide.

"Yeah, the Bar-C encompasses much of the county. But not the town, of course. And there're also a couple of smaller ranches nearby that we don't own—yet."

"And you've lived here all your life?"

So, she had a few questions, too. "Yes, ma'am. Born and raised."

"Then you probably know most of the people who live here. Right?"

Now, that was an odd question. Suddenly he felt as if he was being interrogated.

"Most of them." His forehead wrinkled up as he tried to think. "There're probably a few dozen cowpokes, who work for the Bar-C or one of the other spreads, that I only know by sight. But I suspect I know by name about ninety-five percent of everyone who lives in Chance County."

She looked intent, as if that was the most important information she'd ever heard. He was about to ask why she was interested when Macy came to the table with menus.

He set aside his questions for the time being so he could make sure she was well fed. But he made up his mind that Summer Wheeler was not leaving this café until she gave him a few answers of her own.

Chapter 2

"You don't have to buy me dinner, Mr. Chance," Summer muttered in her most determined, independent voice.

But Travis ignored her, lifting his chin at the café owner's raised eyebrows, as if to say, "Pay no attention to what this woman says, and do what I tell you." The arrogant man had already placed an order for Summer. Nicely, of course. Saying something to the effect that he knew better what the café served. As though someone she had only known for a couple of hours could automatically judge her preferences.

"Just put it on my bill, Macy," he said with authority.

A harried-looking Macy nodded silently and charged off toward the kitchen. It seemed the woman who owned the café was yet another person in this town who treated Mr. Travis Chance with deference. Summer began to look at him a little differently, too.

If she hadn't been so hungry all of a sudden, she would've insisted on paying for her own dinner. She wasn't altogether crazy about this guy asserting his almighty power by assuming what she wanted and could afford. And besides, she still had enough cash left to buy a meal or two.

There was a time when she would've let him have it for his assumptions. But that was before. Before the lost years, when she would rather have died than take another breath. Those endless days, months, years when she'd wished she could disappear from the face of the earth. When eating, sleeping—existing—were just too much to bear. She'd been close to a black abyss during that time, and continued breathing today only because she was too much of a coward to end it all.

Outside the café's windows, the storm raged and beat rain against the glass. Inside, she tried to still her tormented mind. A few months ago she'd finally arrived at a kind of truce with herself. She'd put one foot in front of the other and lived. Lived each day as it came.

Today the chance of finding one of the men who'd sent her to the edge of hell was all that was keeping her alive. And she almost had him. Had actually *seen* him driving by.

"Call me Travis," he said, bringing her back to the moment. "Everyone does. There're far too many Mr. Chances in this town. It gets confusing if we're all called by the same name."

Without warning, he stood and stepped beside her chair, holding out his hands. "May I help you with your pack and jacket? It's too warm in here to be saddled with a coat."

She squirmed out of her pack and let him help with her slightly damp, lightweight jacket. "Thanks, uh…Travis."

He set her pack on the empty seat at the table and placed both their coats on a coat tree in the corner. Within moments he was back at the table.

He'd stood, walked and sat like a man in perfect balance, in tune with his surroundings. She envied him the ability to seem so at ease with himself. And the charge she got from just watching such a sexy man unnerved her.

In order to defer any questions he might ask, she had one or two of her own ready. "So, you said 'a lot of Chances.' You have a big family?"

A slight frown crossed his face and a deep sadness crept into his eyes. "There were six kids in my family. Five boys. I'm the second oldest. My littlest brother died when he was ten, and one of my other brothers is off God-only-knows-where right now. That still leaves three of us by the name of Chance living in the area."

He hadn't mentioned anything about the sixth kid—a sister. And Summer's instincts told her it would be best to stay away from too many touchy, personal questions before she knew more about his background.

"Did I hear you tell Mrs. Murphy that your wife was out of town?" She knew that wasn't what she'd overheard, but it was as good a way as any to find out if he was married. That couldn't be a too touchy, too personal question, could it?

He took a sip of water. "Not my wife. My housekeeper."

Well, damn, he'd wiggled out of answering. "Okay, I'll ask outright. Are you married?"

It was a more direct question than she'd asked anyone in years. But she'd been making quite a lot of changes to the dried-up, empty person she used to be. The question must have something to do with that nothing-to-lose attitude she'd developed recently.

Another look, one she couldn't name, flitted across his

eyes and replaced the sadness. "I'm divorced. Raising a little girl on my own. A single dad."

Oh. Thank God he hadn't said he was a widower. Hadn't she just told herself not to ask potentially touchy questions? And then the first thing she'd done was walk right off that cliff. She was lucky.

"Are *you* married?" His gaze narrowed on her for the moment.

Okay, now, *there* was the real reason she should refrain from asking the personal questions. They always came back to bite her.

"I'm a widow." Her voice sounded surprisingly strong and clear. She must be getting better at answering that one.

"I'm sorry." He moved a hand as though starting to lay it across one of hers in comfort.

Dreading the question that typically came next, she quickly put both her hands in her lap and tried to head him off. "No need. It's been a long time."

"Really? You look too young to have been a widow for a long time."

Macy came back to the table with their plates right then, so Summer didn't feel compelled to make a comment. But he was bound to want more answers eventually, and she steeled herself to give them. She also had to be more careful about her casual conversations. She was piling up a load of questions about this guy that she knew better than to ask.

He dug quietly into his heaping plate of brisket, and she found herself staring while she slowly chewed her own meal. He ate with gusto and purpose. Fascinated by the restrained power she saw in his hands, in the whole of his body, she couldn't help noticing more details about the man.

The strong jaw. A long and very masculine neck, leading to wide shoulders, and on down to bunching biceps under his long-sleeved shirt. Pure power—held in check.

His every movement seemed designed to be competent, grounded and proficient. A tingle of something in her gut that she hadn't felt in a long, long time caught her off guard. She had to wonder if he made love with the same kind of proficiency and competence as he ate a meal.

Uh, stop. Delete that thought. What was the matter with her?

Still obsessed with the memories of two dark shadows coming out of her nightmares to destroy her whole world, she had no emotional energy left to start a serious relationship with anyone. She must put aside those kinds of thoughts until she could erase the incapacitating memories for good. And the only way to do it was to see that the last of those shadows received the justice he deserved.

Or she would die trying. That's the very reason she'd come here.

"Enjoying the barbecue?" He'd looked up to find her staring.

"Yes, very much." She took another bite.

She wanted this man to like her. Badly. A strong and sexy man, he also seemed kind and generous. Besides, she thought he might be persuaded to help her without really knowing all the reasons behind it. After all, he was a powerhouse in this town, and if she was going to stay here long enough to accomplish her mission and find her man, she would need him in her corner.

Taking those thoughts a little further, she realized it sounded a lot like she would be deceiving him *and* using him. Such things really were not like her. It wasn't who she was. Usually. Or maybe it wasn't who she used to be.

But desperate times called for desperate measures. She

picked around her plate, thoughtfully and carefully, trying to decide how much to reveal.

He pushed back his plate and asked the question she'd known was coming. "You look so young. Did your husband die in the service?"

"No. Actually, it was a horrific tragedy, but it took place over five years ago. I went through a lot afterward, but I've gotten a handle on myself now. I've decided to completely change my life. That's what I'm doing in Texas. Looking for a new place to settle."

Only a small white lie, but it seemed to do what she'd hoped. Sympathy jumped into his eyes as he picked up his glass for a drink of water. If she were lucky, he wouldn't push her any further.

"Then I'm glad you got lost in our neck of the woods. Otherwise, we might never have met. And I think we're going to become friends."

Well, that's what she wanted. Sort of. But she wasn't sure what he'd meant about this "friends" thing. Did he mean friends with no fringe benefits? Or did he mean friends with no secrets?

One way or the other, she figured she was in big trouble.

Travis watched the young woman's burning blue eyes closely. Something she'd told him seemed to be bothering her. He prided himself on being a good judge of people, and she was not telling him the whole truth.

People did that all the time. Lied about little things. But whatever this was, it seemed to make her squirm.

Without having known her for long, he came to the conclusion that here was a basically good woman. Vulnerable after a tragic life event, to be sure. And afraid of something—perhaps from her past. But good, deep down.

He wasn't sure why he felt so strongly about that. But his instincts were seldom wrong.

At the front register, Macy finished ringing up the checks of the two cowpokes. After they left, she came to the table to ask if they wanted dessert.

"I'd like a little of your homemade pecan pie, Mace." He turned to Summer. "Have you left room to join me? Macy makes the best pie."

She nodded and looked up at Macy. "Just a small piece, please."

Macy pushed the hair off her face and sighed. "Sure thing. But I'm afraid I don't have any vanilla ice cream for à la mode. I'm kinda backed up tonight. Is that okay?"

Both he and Summer nodded, as Macy gathered their empty plates and headed off to the kitchen.

"She certainly looks like she could use some help. Even tonight when there aren't that many customers. Is it ever busy in here?"

"You should see this place at breakfast. Lines out the door. But I'm guessing her hubby didn't make it in to work tonight. He's the cook, but he's also a disabled veteran. Some days the pain in his back and leg gets to be too much for him."

Summer frowned and looked down at her hands. He expected her to say something else, but she remained silent.

"A penny for your thoughts." To his own ears the familiar sentence sounded like what it was, a terrible and ancient saying and one he never used, but it was all he could come up with.

It did the trick, though, and brought her head up. "I don't think my thoughts are worth a penny. I was just wondering if Macy might need some help."

Of course, he should have realized. "You're looking for work?"

"Temporarily. I'll need to earn enough money to fix my car."

He sat back, his mind racing. He couldn't just hand her the money. She had too much pride for that. It had been everything he could do to convince her to let him pay for her supper.

"I'm afraid Macy wouldn't be able to afford any more help right now," he began slowly. "We're heading into winter, the slowest time of year. I'm sure she's pulling this quiet night by herself to save money, not for lack of available workers."

"Oh." Summer's eyes were so expressive, her disappointment clear and compelling. He could sit and watch the emotions play across her face all night.

"But I might have an idea." Yeah, this idea might actually work to convince her to take help from him. "My daughter is seven—uh—going on thirty. She's a handful. And my housekeeper is getting married in a month and up to her neck making plans and attending parties. We could sure use a little extra help around the house during this hectic time. Would you consider giving us a hand? The pay would probably be just enough to fix that car of yours."

Instead of the grateful smile he'd hoped to see, a look of pure dismay broke out on her face. "Um, I don't know. Your daughter is seven?"

That was her sticking point? She didn't like children? Impossible. She was too gentle. Something about her just said she'd make a terrific mother. Maybe it was because she reminded him of his own mother. Summer must like kids. So that couldn't be it.

"Jenna is very grown-up for her age," he argued. "And you don't have to pick up after her—much."

"Well, maybe." Summer's expressive face told him she

wanted to leap at the offer, but something was holding her back.

Macy arrived with their pie.

"Tell you what," he began, as Macy set a plate before her. "Why don't you come on out to the ranch with me and Jenna tonight? We've got lots of room. Take a day or two to get to know her and the household, and see what you think? I know our housekeeper would be most grateful for anything you can do to help."

Macy set his pie plate down and turned to Summer. "You going to work for Travis? You won't be sorry. He's a terrific boss. Rosie had a devil of a time deciding whether to get married and leave town or keep the best housekeeping job in the state."

Travis felt his face flush at the unsolicited compliment. But he finally saw what he'd hoped to see earlier. Summer's lips tilted up in her first genuine smile since he'd met her.

"All right," she said as she picked up her fork. "I guess giving it a try for a couple of days wouldn't hurt anything."

Good. He might as well do something that would help them both out at the same time. He needed a housekeeper and she needed a job. Simple. He was determined to be of service to this young woman—no matter that he would probably be accused of controlling and meddling again.

He didn't have any doubts that, once she met Jenna and Rosie and saw the ranch, all her fears would subside. He intended to give her a helping hand, whether she wanted one or not, and in the meantime, maybe he'd get to know her a whole lot better.

By the time they went back to the garage and picked up her things, the storm had subsided, but Summer's hands were trembling. Could she do this? Could she meet and befriend a seven-year-old girl?

Her own sweet Emma would've been almost six by now. Just thinking her baby's name gave Summer an ache in the chest that nearly doubled her over.

She'd tried to stay out of situations where children could be involved, for all of the endless last five years. Even though her fondest wish growing up had been to work with and have her own kids.

The lonely years of her childhood, with parents who claimed to love her but left her with nannies and in boarding schools, came looming out of her mind. How she'd longed for a sister or brother, any kind of friend or family. She'd vowed to find a career that involved children and to have at least six of her own.

And she'd thought she'd made a good start. Emma was so sweet and precious. Summer had been ready to have another child as soon as possible.

Until everything blew up in her face, blowing her dreams away in a puff of smoke.

"Jenna's not far," Travis said from the driver's seat as they left the garage. "Just on the other side of town. She's been staying with my aunt June while Rosie is off on a shopping trip. I'm sure the two of you will get along real well."

Yeah? Summer wasn't so sure. In fact, the more she thought about it, the more she came to the conclusion that she might not be cut out for taking care of kids at this point in her life. Oh, a baby she probably could've managed. But a girl who could talk and dream and play with dolls, as Summer had always imagined Emma would do? Not so much.

Fidgeting in her seat, she said, "I don't have any experience with seven-year-olds. I'd be better off taking over the household chores for your Rosie, and letting her take care of your daughter."

Travis smiled in a benevolent manner. "Nonsense. Jenna's no trouble. She may be a little headstrong, but she's sweet and kind to a fault. You'll see. Everyone falls in love with her within five minutes of meeting her."

Summer bit her lip as they pulled into the front yard of a two-story, clapboard house. A little girl with long blond pigtails came running down the porch steps, a backpack slung over her shoulder.

"Hey, Daddy," she called out as she neared the SUV. "You're kinda late. I need to get home to check on Measles. She's expecting her baby tonight."

Travis jumped out of the SUV, but he wasn't fast enough to stop the girl. She threw open the front passenger door and reared back to toss her pack up into the seat before getting in. But when Jenna spotted Summer in the front seat, she stopped and narrowed her eyes.

"Who are you? What are you doing in my place?"

"Jenna!" Travis arrived and took her pack. "That's no way to say hello. This is Summer Wheeler, and we're hoping to hire her to help Rosie out for the next month or so. We're all going to be friends."

The girl harrumphed and threw her hands on her hips. "Tell her to get in the back, Daddy. I ride up front."

"Jenna." Travis's voice sounded disbelieving. "You just started riding in front a couple of months ago, when you hit seven. You can sit in your old place in back for one night."

He opened the back and tossed her backpack in. "Hop up if you want to see Measles so badly."

Little Jenna didn't look too pleased, but she climbed into the backseat and buckled herself in. As Travis drove off, Summer tried to calm her pounding heart. The little one was the exact image of how she'd always imagined her daughter would've looked at this age.

But the girl didn't seem any happier to have a new adult in her life than Summer was to have a child in hers.

"Daddy," she said grumpily as they left the town behind and rode out through open ranch land, "does *she* know how to ride?"

"Her name is Summer, Jenna. And I don't know. Why don't you ask her?"

Without a change in tune, Jenna piped up, "Well, *do* you?"

"If you mean horses, I'm afraid not. But maybe you can teach me."

"You don't know how to ride? What *do* you know?"

Summer was at a loss for words, so she remained quiet.

"Daddy, I don't want her. We don't need anyone. Send her away."

"That's not nice, Jenna. Behave. She stays."

Jenna folded her arms over her chest and sighed. "Oh, brother. This is just awful. It's not going to work out at all."

Chapter 3

Summer agreed with the little girl. This wasn't going to work out well at all.

But try telling that to Travis. He'd set his jaw and thrown his daughter one last steely gaze.

As they rode in the SUV through the darkened countryside, she reminded herself that it would probably be a good thing if Jenna didn't want her company. The child's attitude could make a perfect excuse for Summer to keep her distance and look for other ways to help out at the ranch. At least, while she searched for her man.

Still, it hurt. Somewhere deep down, when Jenna first appeared on the porch steps, Summer had immediately wanted some kind of relationship with her. Summer wasn't exactly sure what she'd hoped for, but the sudden opportunity to be the girl's caretaker had triggered a desire far down in her subconscious. It had been a huge surprise.

But looking at things logically, if she refrained from

becoming involved in the little girl's daily life, it would be better for everyone all the way around. Emotionally, however, it stung just as if someone had offered a piece of chocolate cake only to snatch it away again.

She'd better get ahold of herself. Slipping backward emotionally wasn't any way to get want she needed. That would only gain her a one-way ticket back to the psychologist's couch.

Silence reigned in the SUV for the next thirty minutes. "How far is it? I thought your ranch was right around here somewhere."

Travis threw her a big grin. "We've been on ranch property for the last twenty minutes. We're almost to the house now. It'll take a while for you to get used to the distances in Texas."

Holy moly. That must be some ginormous ranching operation they had going on here.

She stared out the window at the black void, wondering if the place was as prosperous as it sounded. "Who runs everything? Your father?"

"See, Daddy?" a voice popped up from behind them. "She's just dumb."

"Jenna! If you don't keep quiet and behave, you will go straight to bed when we get home." Travis cleared his throat. "Sorry about that. I think Jenna must be overly tired. She's usually a very *kind* and helpful little girl."

A dead silence reverberated from the backseat.

"But in answer to your question," he said, turning his chin toward her for the moment. "My dad passed away nearly ten years ago. I'm the CEO of the family corporation. I don't do it all alone, of course. There's lots of help. And recently, that help includes one of my brothers. Nice to have more family involved, but I guess you could say I make most of the tough decisions alone."

"That must be a big job."

"Somebody has to make things happen."

Just then the car's headlights illuminated a big, fancy gate with BAR-C emblazoned in scrollwork at the top. Travis slowed the SUV and punched a button on the dashboard. The gates opened slowly.

"Pretty fancy." She was surprised when the words she'd thought tumbled from her mouth.

"We still have plenty of gates throughout the ranch that need to be opened by hand."

"Oh, I didn't mean…" She wasn't sure what she'd meant. Just that she should've kept her mouth shut.

"Gates on a working cattle ranch are required for more than privacy," he informed her. "They're used to keep the animals where we want them, instead of wandering out of the pastures and onto the roads. Cattle guards are used for the same reason on unfenced land. Wait until you drive over one of those babies. You won't forget the experience."

"Daddy, hurry up."

A dangerous pause from the front seat, along with a quick glare that only a stern father could give, kept Jenna quietly bouncing in her seat as they headed up a long drive. Curving around a circle to the front door of a mansion that looked like it belonged in one of those expensive suburbs where Summer had come from, the SUV finally pulled to a stop. This place just screamed money. Suddenly she felt uncomfortable.

Her in-laws had lived in a house like this one. Her parents had, too—whenever they'd been at home and not traveling. She'd sworn to herself that, when she had a choice, her homes would be cozy, intimate. Not big and ostentatious. Not like this one.

But her husband had seen things the opposite way.

He'd wanted his surroundings—his car, his clothes, his home—to proclaim his wealth to the world. And in the end, that public declaration was what killed him.

Well, that and being born into the wrong family.

"Look, Jenna." Travis put the SUV in park and shut it down. "Rosie's back early." Unbuckling, he climbed out.

Young Jenna unbuckled herself too, and sprang out of the backseat before the engine even stopped purring. Summer took a breath, trying to support shaky nerves, then eased her feet to the driveway and followed Jenna and Travis up the steps, toward the woman waiting at the door.

Sneaking a peek at the housekeeper as she climbed the porch stairs, Summer was surprised to see a woman of nearly fifty. She'd thought of the housekeeper as a young woman—probably because of her impending marriage.

Regardless of her age, Rosie's soft eyes and gentle smile made her seem like a genuinely kind person. Summer just hoped that kindness would extend to a stranger coming to take over part of her job.

"I'm so glad you're home." Jenna threw her arms around the older woman's waist.

"Hello to you, too," Rosie said with a laugh. "You're a little late coming home. Measles already had her foal. You'll have to hurry if you want to see the filly before your bedtime."

"A girl? Measles had a girl? Oh, boy." Jenna dropped her backpack on the tile floor in the foyer and dashed off toward the back of the house.

Travis's chuckle from behind her made Summer turn around. "Jenna's not usually this scattered and impolite," he said with a grimace. "She's a little overly excited tonight about the new foal, because I told her this one would be hers eventually."

Summer nodded. Horses were a little out of her area of expertise. But she could understand the emotions of a child getting something she'd been looking forward to for a long time.

Taking her by the elbow, Travis turned his head to speak to his housekeeper. "Rosie, this is Summer Wheeler. She's in a tough spot. Her car broke down and she needs to earn extra cash to have it fixed. You think you can find a few chores to keep her busy?"

Rosie's deep brown eyes sparked with interest. "Are you kidding? That's perfect. You know there're always things need doing around here. An extra pair of hands means I can have more time to finish my dress and work on the wedding details."

It was Travis's turn to nod his head. "Uh-huh. Well, why don't you fix Summer up in one of the upstairs guest rooms and get her settled? I think I'd better head for the barn to check on Jenna before she drags that foal into bed with her."

Rosie was chuckling under her breath as Travis turned to address Summer. "Rosie will make sure you have everything you need for tonight. And I'll see you at breakfast." He released her elbow. "Oh, and we're real glad to have you helping out on the Bar-C." With that, he headed off into the shadows of a dark night.

She watched him disappear, wondering how she'd ever gotten mixed up with anyone so...so larger than life.

"Yeah, he's a pistol, all right," Rosie said as she touched her arm. "You can sure see where Jenna gets her spunk. But don't think he isn't itching to see that foal the same as Jenna. New life on the ranch is always a miracle."

Summer turned to the older woman and blinked back whatever inappropriate thoughts she'd been having. About

Travis. About Jenna. And now about new life. Obviously they showed on her face.

"Come on in," Rosie said with a deep twang. "Let's go up, pick you out a nice room and make you comfortable. Days start early around here, and you need a good night's sleep if you intend to help me keep up with that little bundle of energy."

Summer didn't want to stop her to point out that she wasn't there to help with Jenna, but to lend a hand with the housekeeping. It just didn't seem very hospitable to contradict her new boss. But just as soon as they got to know each other a little better, she would straighten Rosie out as to her duties.

In very short order, Rosie chose a nice room that had already been made up and showed her to the nearest bathroom facilities, right next door. "You think you'll be okay here?" she asked.

"Better than okay. Thanks. This is really nice of you. I'm sorry Travis didn't give you a heads-up that I was coming before we just arrived on your doorstep."

Rosie waved her off. "Oh, that's Travis's way. He's a decent man who tends to jump into situations before he thinks them all the way through. Especially when he sees a need. I'm used to him doing things like that. Been working for him since he first brought his bride home. Over ten years now, I guess it's been."

Summer was curious and let her mouth run when, no doubt, she should've kept it shut. "Does Jenna see her mom often? Do they share custody?"

Rosie didn't seem to mind the rather nosy questions, but her expression turned melancholy. "No. I sincerely doubt Jenna would remember what her mother looks like. She wasn't even two yet when Callie took off. And that cold-hearted mother of hers never looked back at the family she'd left behind—not once. She just took off for the bright lights of Nashville. Fancied herself a singer, you know."

"So Jenna never sees her?"

"Never. Poor little thing waits by the mailbox around her birthday, hoping for some word. But Callie never bothers with presents or cards. To my knowledge, she's only called her own daughter twice in the whole five years she's been gone."

Summer's stomach clenched at the thought of a mother who'd apparently thrown away a relationship with her child. Life seemed so unfair, when Summer would gladly give up five years of her life, along with her right arm, for a chance to have a relationship with her own daughter.

"I didn't mean to make you sad about Jenna's situation." Rosie lowered her voice and shook her head slowly. "Travis sees to it his girl has all the love and friendship a child could ever want. If you're still around for Christmas, you'll see. The fiestas for Jenna go on for days."

Fiestas, presents and friends—even a wonderful, loving father didn't make up for having no mother. Summer knew that and felt empathy for the little girl. No wonder Jenna was standoffish with strangers. Especially women. She hadn't had the best experience with the most important woman in her life up until now.

It didn't take long for Rosie to leave Summer alone in the room. In minutes she'd changed into her nightgown and found herself lying in bed, looking at the ceiling, deep in thought. But it wasn't Jenna she was thinking about. It wasn't even baby Emma, gone these last five years, who captured her attention tonight.

Nope. It was the arrogant man with a big-as-Texas heart and a smile in his eyes, even when he was dead serious, that kept her tossing in bed this time.

She had a sneaking suspicion Travis would turn into either the biggest obstacle in her path or the easiest way of getting what she wanted the most: the man she'd been hunting.

Travis walked into the kitchen long before sunrise to grab a quick cup a coffee. But the first thing he saw stopped him cold.

"Morning, Travis." Summer threw him a quick smile and went back to work over the stove. "Coffee's ready, and I'll have eggs Benedict and waffles on the table in a few minutes."

He turned to Rosie, who was setting the table, with a quirked eyebrow. She glanced up and silently shook her head as if to say, "This isn't my doing."

After pouring himself a mug of fresh coffee, he sauntered over to the stove. "It smells delicious, but you don't have to cook. Especially breakfast. We usually get by on coffee and rolls until our big, noontime dinner. You should still be in bed getting your rest."

"I don't need rest. I need to stay busy. And cooking is my pleasure. What's more, a good breakfast is the most important meal of the day. Have a seat. It's ready."

Travis gave up trying to challenge the tornado shoveling food onto the table. As he watched her, he noticed her movements seemed almost frenzied. As though, if she stopped moving, she might collapse. Or perhaps as if, when she stopped, she would be forced to face whatever was bothering her.

"Are you going to join me?" He worked to keep his tone low, calm.

"Yes, in a moment. Rosie, there's plenty for you, too. Sit down and eat."

"Oh. Uh...I usually wait to eat with Jenna."

"I'll be happy to make Jenna's breakfast when she comes down. What does she usually like to eat in the morning?"

"Cereal and toast. She's a bit of a picky eater."

Summer *tsk*ed and frowned. "That's not a very sound way to start the day. Would she eat scrambled eggs and waffles if I made them?"

"Maybe. I'm not sure."

"Great." Summer sat at an empty place. "We'll give that a try when she gets up."

Turning to him, Summer raised her eyebrows. "Have you tasted anything yet? I hope you like the food. I thought about making huevos rancheros, but I was afraid you might not care for anything spicy this early. Nearly everyone likes my eggs Benedict, though."

Still reeling from the idea of having his beautiful new employee prepare food for them, he took a bite. "Good. How'd you learn to cook like this?"

"I took gourmet classes once—in my other life. It was a fun hobby."

Her other life? Interesting way to put it. It made him more curious than ever about what she'd been through to arrive in Chance, Texas.

"Well, I guess if it makes you happy, Rosie probably won't mind if you take over her cooking duties for a while. But…"

He interrupted his sentence when he heard the sound of heavy boot-falls coming across the hardwood floor in the living room. Turning, he expected to see either his foreman Barrett or his older brother Sam coming to talk about ranch business.

It turned out it wasn't either one of the two.

"Morning, all. Geez, it smells good in here. What's the

occas…?" His younger brother, Gage, stopped walking and talking when he spotted Summer at the table.

"Morning, brother." Travis tilted his head toward Summer. "This is Summer Wheeler. She'll be helping Rosie out around here for a while. At least until the wedding and we can locate someone more permanent to look after Jenna."

Next, Travis turned his attention to Summer. "This suddenly-struck-dumb idiot is my younger brother, Gage Chance. He's a private investigator and has never shown up at such an early hour in his whole life. I think something must've affected his manners—or his brain."

Summer was on her feet in an instant. But she looked terrified, nervous and unsure of herself. "Nice to meet you. Can I fix you something? Waffles? Eggs Benedict?"

Gage blinked a couple of times before speaking. "Ah, no, thanks. But I will have one of those mugs of coffee." After pouring himself a cup, he turned one of the high-backed chairs around and straddled it, leaning his elbows across the back.

"What are you doing out and about this early, Gage?"

"I'm always up before the sun. I was raised on the Bar-C, same as you. Our old man was a tough taskmaster. No sleeping in when there's work to be done, according to Cameron Chance. But I don't usually have business on the ranch that won't wait for daybreak."

"Okay. What's so danged important this morning?"

Gage rolled his eyes and blew across the top of his coffee. "I finally got a lead on Cami."

Travis straightened his spine and sat up. "When? Where?"

"That got your attention, didn't it? You know I've been finishing up a client's case on the West Coast for the last week. Well, while I was that close, I decided to do a little more digging around in L.A. And I found a woman who was employed by the California Department of Social Services during the years when Cami was placed for adoption."

"So we know for sure she went through some kind of formal adoption procedure?"

Gage set his mug down and rose. "Let's take this into your office. I'll show you what I learned on the internet."

Throwing his napkin on the table, Travis stood too and turned to Rosie and Summer. "Thanks for the breakfast. You do good work. Rosie, show her what you need done."

He started to follow Gage out the door, then turned back. "If she's interested, give Summer a rundown on Cami, so she won't be wondering what's going on. And bring her out to the ranch office before noon, and we'll show her the operation."

Rosie nodded. "Sure thing. Have a good morning. We'll handle things here."

Trailing his brother to his home-office computer, Travis's mind was torn. He was curious about what had happened with his brother's investigation into their missing sister's whereabouts, but also wished he could spend the day with Summer, getting to know her better. The whole Chance family had been looking for Cami for years, and every lead had turned to a dead end. He didn't want his hopes raised too high. But for now, he would give Gage his complete attention.

When they entered the office and shut the door behind them, Gage had something else to say first. "All right. Who is she? Where did you meet her?"

"Summer? I ran into her at Stockard's garage. Her car broke down, and she needs to earn the cash to have it repaired. Seems like a nice enough gal."

"Nice? What do you know about her background? She

could be running from the law. Or she could be one of those women on the make for an unsuspecting male to sink her hooks into. You can't just go around picking up strangers and bringing them into your home. You have a child to consider."

Travis felt his anger building and tried to clamp down on it. After all, his brother was only worried about his welfare. Still…

"I'm not like you, Gage. I don't automatically think the worst of people. And most times, I'm right."

Plopping down at his desk, Travis waved his brother into the other chair. "Summer told me she came from back east and that she'd had a family tragedy about five years ago that took the life of her husband. Said it nearly killed her but she's on the mend and looking for a change. I have no reason not to believe her."

"That's it? That's all you know?"

"What else do I need?" The minute the words were uttered, Travis realized he did need more. That she'd been holding something back. But he wanted her to volunteer the information.

"Mind if I do a little digging into her background? I'll be discreet."

Travis suffocated a heavy sigh. "All right. But I want to know immediately if you find something rotten or illegal. No calling the cops before you talk to me. Deal?"

Gage agreed. But Travis knew it didn't matter what he said. There was no way to stop Gage once he'd made up his mind.

All of a sudden his simple, good deed for the lovely widow with spectacular blue eyes was turning into something much more complicated. Dang it, anyway.

Chapter 4

"So, what time does Jenna come down for breakfast?" Summer stood at the sink doing dishes and thinking about what she could cook that would please a child of seven.

"Usually she's down within minutes of when we have to leave for school." Rosie dried a dish and put it away. "And I have to drive her, because she's never on time for the bus. But she's managing to dress herself and brush her own teeth and hair these days. That's a big improvement."

Summer was thinking of going upstairs to see what she could do to speed up the process, but then remembered that she hadn't wanted to get too involved with the girl. She'd be better off sticking to cooking and cleaning.

And while she was at it, maybe she should find out more about Travis. "Rosie, what happened to Travis and Gage's sister?"

Rosie raised her eyebrows and scrunched up her mouth.

"In order for that to make sense, I'll need to tell you the whole family history. It's complicated, but I'll try to make it as brief as possible. Jenna will be here in a minute, and we'll have to hustle to get her to school on time."

"Okay. And that helps me decide what I'm fixing for Jenna to eat. Waffles with peanut butter and jelly it is. She can wolf them down on the way to school. Can I work while you talk?"

"Go right ahead. I'll finish the dishes." Rosie picked up a dry dish towel. "First, you have to know that when the Chance children were fairly young—Travis was only seventeen—their mother was found murdered in her own home. The sheriff eventually arrested their father for the crime, and he went to prison."

"You sound like you don't believe he did it." Summer poured the batter into the waffle iron while she listened.

"No one in the family believes he was guilty. But the Chance siblings were all too young to do much about proving their theories back then. And years later, all the evidence was lost or covered over. Anyway, five years after he was sentenced, their father was murdered by another inmate while in prison."

Rosie paused a moment to put dishes in a cupboard. "After their mother's murder, the Chance kids decided to run the ranch on their own. The oldest was only nineteen, and they soon learned the place was loaded down with lots of debts and problems. It was everything the two oldest boys could do to hold things together and watch after the younger kids. So, when their mother's sister volunteered to take the baby girl into her home, Travis and his older brother, Sam, jumped at the chance, to give the little girl a better life than she would've had with a bunch of young men, who knew nothing about what a girl needs."

"Weren't there a lot of relatives nearby that could've pitched in?"

"Actually, no. Their grandparents were gone by then, and their father's only remaining sister was living in New York. Besides, the boys loved their maternal aunt and thought their mother had loved her, too. She lived right in Chance, close by, and they believed her home would be the best thing for their sister. What they didn't know was that their aunt had a drug problem. Within weeks she disappeared, taking their four-year-old baby sister with her."

"Oh, my gosh. That's terrible." Summer felt a chill run down her arms. It took a supreme act of will to keep cooking and listening. She would rather not hear about anything so terrible. But she'd asked, so she hung in and listened.

"Yeah, it was real hard on the boys. The sheriff called in the FBI, of course, but all their searches were useless. The authorities managed to trace the aunt's movements to Southern California, but after that it was like she and the girl had been swallowed up by a black hole. Gone."

"How awful for the family. Did they ever find out anything else?" With her hands full of jars of peanut butter and jelly, Summer used her wrists to shove aside the unwanted wetness on her cheeks.

"About five years later, the aunt's body showed up in a San Diego morgue. Dead of an overdose. But there was never any trace of the little sister."

"Hey!" Jenna's high-pitched voice suddenly reverberated off the kitchen tiles, as she bounded into the room and stared at the empty table. "Where's my cereal?"

Rosie laughed as she turned to the little girl. "You're late. As usual. But Summer has made something good for you to eat on the way to school. Grab your backpack and let's go."

"Do you mind if I go along?" Summer was eager to ride back into town. "I can finish the cleanup after we drop Jenna off." She wanted to take every opportunity to search for her man.

It would be so easy if she knew which alias he might be using. The P.I. she'd hired told her the guy had been known in prison by the name of Hoss. And the name he'd used with the mob was Bobby Packard. But he'd been known to use at least a dozen others, so those wouldn't help her here.

"No," Jenna said in a huff.

"Sure," Rosie said at the same time, then turned to glare at Jenna. "Mind your manners, little girl. What difference does it make if Summer comes with us?"

"Well, I get the front seat."

Summer had to chuckle, but she tried not to let it show. "Not a problem for me. I'll be glad to take the backseat." She grabbed a bunch of paper towels and the waffle sandwiches. "I spotted juice boxes in the fridge. Want to grab one for the ride?"

Jenna scowled at the suggestion, but pulled open the refrigerator door and took out an orange juice anyway. "What'd you make me to eat?" She slammed the door and grabbed her backpack.

"It's a surprise. But I hope you like it."

"Probably not." Jenna ran for the kitchen door. "Let's go. If I'm late, I'll tell Ms. Dowd it was your fault."

Rosie silently shook her head, picked up a set of keys from the board next to the back door, and proceeded Jenna outside.

Summer sighed, moving to follow them on heavy feet.

This little girl's attitude was not at all like her daydreams
of a seven-year-old daughter.

Regardless of her bad attitude, Jenna had become a
challenge. Deep inside, this child was in pain—hurting in
just the same way as Summer. In fact, she felt continual
pain at the spot where she wore a bruise in place of her
heart.

Maybe, if she could do something to help Jenna, she
could also lessen her own pain. Anyway, it might be worth
a shot. All of a sudden, Jenna seemed worth the trouble.

Grumpy and tired, Travis dropped out of the cockpit
of his Cessna to the night-cooled asphalt of the Bar-C's
airstrip and headed for his truck, parked at the hangar.
It had been a hell of a few days. Instead of his original
plans, he'd been called to the state capital for an emergency meeting with the agriculture secretary.

It seemed the rainstorm they'd had had done nothing to
stem the severe drought in the rest of the state. The Bar-C
lands were in no trouble, but ranchers in the Panhandle
were suffering. Travis had agreed to pool resources to
help them out.

They'd come up with a decent emergency plan, but
it had taken too long. And he'd been looking forward to
showing Summer the ranch operations. The horses. The
cattle and the oil fields. Perhaps he might've even driven
her out to the wind-plant operations for a picnic.

Now it was so late he'd missed dinner, and Jenna would
probably already be in bed. The only potential light in his
dreary outlook for the rest of his evening was that Summer
might still be awake.

He wasn't sure what had come over him where she was
concerned. Every time he thought of her, the tension eased
in his gut. But then that low knot magically reappeared

whenever he was actually in her presence. He found himself craving the sight of her after having known her for only a short while.

She was an enigma, stirring him in many ways. Her fragile build couldn't hide the female curves she had in all the right places. He hadn't thought he'd noticed, but they'd haunted his dreams last night.

And those startling blue eyes, as wide as Texas, warmed him whenever he found a way to make her smile, and saddened him when the edges tipped down in a frown. So, yes, he was hot for her in the way a man is stirred by any beautiful female. But this was also different. She was different.

He wanted to know more about her than just that compelling body. He wanted to understand her both inside and out. All her secret places. And all her secret thoughts.

But instinctively he knew that he couldn't pull the information out of her. He wanted to know, but only when the time was right.

Shaking his head, he stepped up into the truck, wondering if he was losing his mind. No woman had bothered him on this level since—ever. His ex, Callie, hadn't gotten to him the way Summer did.

Callie had been a challenge—yes. But she was more a challenge to his ego. She'd been the prettiest girl in school, and everybody had expected them to get together in the end. So, when his older brother went off to the army and he'd had to take charge of the Bar-C, Travis just assumed he and Callie would marry and start a family. He never gave her the chance to say no. And maybe she'd been too young to know she could.

After their relationship crashed and burned, he'd promised himself to never again push someone that hard. It had all been his fault from the beginning. He hadn't given

Callie the opportunity to know her own heart—or what she truly wanted out of life.

And in the end, he'd hurt everyone involved, mostly Jenna, by insisting they marry and start a family right away. Obviously, he knew next to nothing about love and was better off being done with marriage for good.

Of course, he'd certainly had lots of opportunities to remarry over the years since Callie had taken off. He'd even been in a couple of semiserious relationships, which he'd broken off before anyone got hurt.

Everyone he knew kept trying to fix him up. But he refused to make the same mistake twice in his life.

No, Jenna would always be his first priority. He'd sworn to provide her with all the love she'd missed by not having her mama around. And he refused to take any chances on hurting her even worse.

So he had no intention of falling under some kind of romantic spell with Summer. But she'd made him curious. Itchy to know all about her.

Nothing wrong with scratching that itch, was there?

Before he could start up the engine, his cell rang. Gage's number appeared. At this hour?

"What do you need, brother?"

"Hello to you too, Travis. Where are you?"

"Just landed at the airstrip. I'm on my way back to the house."

"I'll meet you there. I've uncovered some intel on Summer's background that I think you should hear."

Travis sat there for a moment, contemplating his feelings. He'd just told himself that he wanted to know more about her. But did he want the info coming from his brother, instead of directly from her?

"All right. But don't come to the house. Meet me at the ranch office in twenty minutes."

Clicking off, Travis turned the key and the pickup roared to life. Gage and his internet searches were a pain in the neck sometimes. But maybe it would be better hearing the facts from him, rather than pushing to get the information from Summer. He wanted to get closer to her—not shove her into a corner the way he had done with his ex-wife.

Gage was already waiting for him by the time he arrived at the ranch office and opened the door. His brother's expression was grim in the ambient glow of the outside floodlights.

"It's late." Flipping on the office's overhead lights, Travis threw his keys on the desk and sat in his favorite chair. "You sure this wouldn't have waited until tomorrow?"

Gage plopped down on the old leather couch opposite him. "I don't need much sleep. And I thought you'd want to know what I found as soon as I confirmed it."

Travis drew a bracing breath. "Please don't tell me she's really an escaped ax murderer. If she's wanted by the law, I don't want to know."

With the most somber smile Travis had ever seen on his younger brother's face, Gage leaned his elbows on his knees. "She's not a criminal. But the police in Greenwich, Connecticut, are quite familiar with her. The detective I spoke to tonight was glad to know she was okay."

"Greenwich? Is that where she's from?"

Gage nodded. "After searching for some kind of tragedy that took place five years ago in the Northeast, I spotted her name in several news accounts and police reports. I hadn't really expected Summer Wheeler to be her real name, but it is."

"Of course it is. She's no liar. I would know that about her."

Gage raised an eyebrow, but continued with his tale. "She may not be a liar, but I have to say she is a master at understatement. That was some family tragedy she had. More like a colossal disaster."

Now Travis's curiosity was reaching a peak. "Quit with the embellishing and give it to me straight."

"Right. It seems your innocent-looking Summer married into one of the biggest mob families in New England. The cop I spoke with says he's convinced she didn't know the truth until it was too late, but I don't find that credible. Hard not to know what business made your in-laws filthy rich."

Shrugging a shoulder, Gage went on, "Anyway, she and her young husband were at home, with their six-month-old daughter asleep in her upstairs nursery, on the night when all hell broke loose. A couple of low-ranking soldiers from a competing mob broke into the house, looking to steal money and then make a hit on their rival's son. They were expecting such a hit would move them up the ranks in their own organization."

Travis felt his chest constrict. But he tried to breathe normally and listen.

"Apparently, one of these dudes was high, and just plain crazy to boot. After they broke in and tied up the husband, the crazy one decided to…uh…take a taste of the young wife. After he roughed her up a little, the other one panicked, locked her away in the basement and took off running. He'd apparently thought he was just involved in a robbery and didn't want any part of what his buddy had in mind."

"How bad was it?"

"No one knows for sure how things went down after

that." Gage blinked a couple of times. "Summer managed to break free of her ties. She didn't know what to do first, but court documents say her only thoughts were of her sleeping child in the upstairs bedroom. She kept hearing terrible noises coming from above her, and finally she began to smell smoke. That's when she used her fists to break a window in the basement and crawled outside."

"Hell."

"Yeah, it must've been for her. The police know she ran next door, half-naked from the earlier abuse and bleeding bad. But by then the fire trucks were already on the way. She turned right around and went back in the house, but she couldn't manage to fight her way upstairs through the smoke and flames. When the paramedics arrived, one of them had to drag her away from the fully engulfed house."

Travis did not want to hear the rest of this, though he knew he had no choice but to sit and listen to the worst. He'd wanted to know her secrets.

"It turned out her husband was dead before the fire was set. And the baby died of smoke inhalation. Summer spent four months in the hospital and in rehab for her burned legs and smoke-filled lungs. Then she was in and out of a psychiatric hospital for the next few years."

Travis could understand her need for mental help. No wonder her eyes burned with intensity sometimes. Like a frightened animal. Now he knew what and who had done that to her.

Clearing his throat, he asked, "Did they catch the creeps that did it?" If not, it would be a struggle not to go after them himself.

"The cops caught up to the crazy one within a few days. He was too stupid to run. The other one apparently was so scared he never stopped running. But, at any rate, it was the crazy one who was the worse of the two. The detective I talked to said they figured the other guy was just a hired hand. He'd actually saved Summer's life by locking her in the basement.

"The creep they caught stood trial, and Summer's testimony convicted him." Gage finished speaking on the end of a breath. "They have the death penalty in Connecticut, but the judge handed him life with no possibility of parole, because there was some question about his mental condition. If the state's lucky, another prisoner in the prison yard will stick the crazy bastard with a shiv someday soon and end it early."

Speechless, Travis hung his head.

"Pretty rough, huh? The cop I talked to seemed surprised that Summer had made it this far without a complete mental breakdown. He said he'd figured she was in the funny farm for good."

"What happened with the husband's parents?" Travis wondered if they had helped Summer.

"The killings started a local mob war, which left an opening for the FBI to gather evidence. Summer's father-in-law is now serving time in a federal pen. Her former mother-in-law committed suicide."

"Then she has no one."

With a giant push, Gage rose to his feet and loomed over him. "Now, don't go doing that again."

"Doing what? What the hell are you talking about?"

"You're feeling sorry for her and convincing yourself you need to take charge of her life. You can't save everyone you meet, brother. The whole world needs saving, and it isn't up to you to do it all."

"Ah, shut up. I know I can't help everyone who needs it. But I can be a friend to those in trouble through no fault of their own, can't I?"

Gage ran his fingers through his hair. "Geez, Trav.

You'd think you didn't have enough on your plate. What are you going to do with a woman on the verge of being a raving nutcase? Start thinking about your family and the ranch first for a change."

"That's not fair. You know my family always comes first." Travis had had enough of Gage's admonitions for the moment. "Go home, bro. You may not need much sleep, but I have to be up in less than five hours for another long day. I appreciate your letting me know about all this. But I'll handle it from here."

Grumbling, Gage turned to leave. "I'll go," he said from the door. "But, remember this—you can't really help her. She needs professional medical care that you know nothing about. Don't say I didn't warn you."

Travis refrained from kicking his brother out the door. He knew Gage was only trying to help. But he was grateful when his brother's truck started up and he was once again alone in his office.

Thinking about the horror story he'd just heard, Travis's heart went out to the young woman who'd lived through the worst of all fates. She'd lost a child.

If the situation were reversed, if he'd lost Jenna like that, he'd be a raving lunatic. And he would probably be wandering around the country just as she was, trying to find peace of mind.

Summer needed someone. She needed him and she needed Jenna. She needed roots and people who cared. And he was going to see that she got just that.

At least for a while.

Chapter 5

Summer leaned against the door frame of Jenna's room and watched Rosie tucking her into bed. It had been a long day, and she wondered if she'd made any headway at all with the little girl.

"Say your prayers, baby." Rosie leaned over and straightened the blanket.

Jenna closed her eyes and folded her hands. "God bless Daddy, Auntie June and all my uncles. And God bless Rosie, Ms. Dowd and my new foal. And, God, please watch out for my mama. She doesn't have anyone to take care of her." Jenna opened her eyes reached out for a hug.

"Didn't you forget someone?" Rosie leaned in and gave her a quick hug. "What about Summer?"

Jenna wrinkled up her nose but quickly closed her eyes and folded her hands. "Dear God, I didn't think I wanted Summer here, but she makes good stuff. She can stay."

Summer held in a gasp and then the tear about to escape

from the corner of her eye, while Rosie turned out the light and shut the door behind her.

"I guess I passed muster today," she whispered to Rosie as they walked down the hall.

"I had a feeling she would eventually respond to you. She really needs people in her life who care about her."

As they walked down the stairs toward the kitchen, Summer asked a question that had been bothering her all day. "I didn't notice any toys in Jenna's room. She has pictures of horses on the walls, and there are ropes and other riding paraphernalia stashed around the room. But I couldn't see any stuffed animals or dolls. Is there a reason for that?"

If Jenna were her little girl, she would have tons of stuffed toys and dolls and doll houses. Emma had at least a dozen soft animals in the few months of her short life. Summer's dreams were full of them now, along with the other dolls she'd been planning to give her child as she grew into them.

Rosie shook her head sadly. "Jenna asked me to put them away several years ago. Said they were too babyish for her. But, in my opinion, it's because dolls and stuffed toys remind her too much of the time before her mother left."

Summer could almost appreciate those sentiments. "What does she think about you leaving?"

"I can feel her pulling away from me. She's protecting herself from another hurt by shutting me out of her life, slowly but surely. I don't like it, but I understand. I wish I could do something to make it better, easier for her, but I don't know what."

"What does Travis think?"

"You'd have to ask him. I suggested once that he needed to remarry for Jenna's sake, and he nearly bit my head off. Said he wouldn't take a chance of hurting his little girl again by getting her hopes too high."

"That's an odd thing to say." It made Summer wonder if Travis had been speaking for himself when he'd mentioned being hurt. And if he was using Jenna as an excuse to protect himself.

Not that it mattered, really. Not to her. She couldn't let herself be interested in applying for the job as Jenna's stepmom. It wouldn't be fair to anyone, in the long run. She'd be afraid of comparing Jenna to her dreams of a lost child. Besides, she'd already blown any chance of a real relationship with Jenna's father by starting off lying to him.

Rosie bid her good-night and went to bed. Summer wasn't the least bit sleepy, so she stayed downstairs, hoping Travis would come back early from his trip. He'd said he would try.

She sat at the kitchen table with a cup of hot milk and thought about her last few days in Chance. After they'd driven Jenna to school that first morning, she'd begged Rosie to drive her through town for a while. Wanting a decent excuse to look for the man she'd seen the first day on her way into town, she'd claimed she needed to learn her way around.

Rosie hadn't minded spending more time in town, saying she had a couple of errands to run anyway. So they'd stopped at a funny old grocery store and picked up supplies, and then they'd gone to a meat processor to retrieve the packaged meats the household had ordered.

During their whole time in town, Summer had kept her eyes trained for any other vehicles. But her mind had wandered. She couldn't stop thinking about Travis. How he was doing, and if he was giving her any thought. Did he wonder about her as she wondered about him?

She'd hoped to spend some time with him when he showed her around the ranch. But he'd phoned Rosie to say he'd been called away, and her hopes at a few moments alone with him were dashed. He hadn't even been able to return for dinner.

She'd told herself the problem wasn't that she was missing him. She couldn't possibly have become so attached to the man so quickly.

She only wanted to seek his opinions about Jenna—to hear his thoughts about how he desired his daughter to be raised. And about a replacement for Rosie when she left to be married. And had he heard anything from the mechanic about her car? She really needed to do something about that car tomorrow.

But all those varying thoughts hadn't stopped her from keeping one eye out for the truck she'd seen. The one carrying the man she sought. It hadn't been at any of the places they'd stopped. So the whole trip to town had been a big waste.

Then, the next afternoon, she and Rosie spent hours cooking and baking. Summer had never seen so much food prepared in one residential kitchen. She'd asked who they were feeding, and Rosie had told her tomorrow was the day of the month Travis always set aside to visit the needy.

Summer couldn't quite picture that, but she went along with everything Rosie did and helped pack the food up for storage in a big walk-in refrigerator. If she were still here next month, she wanted to be able to show the new housekeeper how things should go.

The days had gone by fast enough, but the nights

seemed endless. At midnight, she finally gave up waiting for Travis and went to bed.

Summer woke up before dawn, feeling cranky and tired. She hadn't slept well. It wasn't the bed. The bed was fine—comfortable. The problem stemmed from bad dreams and tossing and turning, worrying about the stupid situation she'd created for herself.

Becoming so involved with the people she'd met in Chance had not been smart. She'd come here for one reason. Not to become entangled in other people's problems.

Rosie was already in the kitchen, washing a few things in the sink, by the time Summer crawled out of bed, took a shower and made it downstairs. But the skies were still gray and the sun not fully up. It made her wonder if Rosie had a hard time sleeping, too.

"Good morning," Rosie said brightly as she handed her a cup of coffee. "Can I fix you something to eat?"

Shaking her head, she replied, "I'll stick to fruit this morning, thanks. It's Saturday—when do you think Jenna will be down? Does she sleep late on weekends?"

Rosie chuckled and poured herself a cup of coffee, too. "Jenna already flew through here about a half hour ago, dragging her father along with her. They were headed to the barn to check on the new foal. She's all excited about naming her little filly.

"I suspect," Rosie said, easing into a chair at the table, "Travis will try to corral her back here for something to eat before too much longer. Saturday is my usual day off, and I have a million things to do."

Rosie folded one knee under her and took a sip of coffee. "Travis takes care of Jenna's meals on the weekends. Or he drops her in town to spend the day with her

great-aunt June. I just stopped in to see if you needed anything. Remember where we stored everything we prepared
yesterday? You can help Travis load it into the SUV, can't
you?"

"Oh, sure. That's not a problem. You have a good day."

Rosie jumped up, a smile lighting up her whole face.
"My fiancé's driving over from San Angelo later. We've
got an appointment with the preacher to go over all the
wedding plans."

"That sounds nice." Summer remembered her wedding,
and how excited she'd been to start her life with the man
she'd thought she loved.

But she'd also had another thought last night and
wanted to test Rosie's response to it. "Uh, are you having
a large wedding? Lots of attendants?"

"Not really. Just my sister, coming down from Dallas
to stand up for me, and we've invited a few friends to be
present. And Travis and Jenna, of course. Why?"

"Have you considered including a flower girl? Or a
young attendant? Anything Jenna can do. I'd thought if
you would involve her more in the wedding, it might help
ease her into the idea of you leaving."

Rosie chuckled but nodded her head. "It's a thought.
I'd just assumed she wouldn't want to do anything so…
girly. But maybe I should ask. If I run into her and Travis
later in town, I'll ask her then."

The next thing Summer knew, Rosie had flung her
arms around her in a big bear-hug. Automatically Summer
pulled back, but Rosie wasn't having any part of that.

Clinging to her for a second, Rosie whispered, "I'm
so glad Travis found you. I think you're going to be real
good for Jenna."

As much as Summer had dreaded being touched for
the last five years, she found herself relaxing into Rosie's

hug. Surprised by her own reactions, Summer bit her lip and found her eyes welling up. Here was a woman she hadn't known long, and she felt more comfortable with her than she had with innumerable old friends back home after the accident. Those *supposed* friends who'd turned away after the tragedy, when they found out about her mob in-laws.

Rosie finally let go and then hustled out the door with a big wave. Not sure what do with all her new emotions, Summer turned and began whipping up breakfast. She'd planned to make something different for Jenna and Travis, and remembering the steps would keep her from thinking too much about anything else.

"If the mama is Measles, why don't we call the baby Mumps?"

Travis followed Jenna through the kitchen door, laughing at his daughter's little joke about the filly's new name. But the moment he spotted Summer standing at the stove, he stopped laughing and held his breath, waiting while his pulse spiked.

Long and thin, Summer's build was slight but still curvy enough to cause his blood to boil. He noticed his fingers curling at the sight of her ash-blond hair hanging down her back in a tempting mass of ringlets. Oh, how he would love to run his hands through that satiny halo in the throes of passion.

Even from behind, Summer made his mouth water.

And then she turned. "Morning. I hope you two are hungry. How was the filly this morning?"

Unable to catch his breath, he stood like a lump and watched Jenna run to Summer's side.

"She's beautiful!" Jenna didn't hug Summer around the

waist as she would have done with Rosie, but she stood
very close to her, waving her arms as she talked.

"The baby's running and eating and everything! I love
her." Jenna suddenly realized something was cooking on
the stove and stood on tiptoe to see what was going on.

"Whoa." Summer dropped her spatula and pulled Jenna
backward. "Careful. The stove is hot. Don't burn yourself."

"What's ya cooking? It smells good."

Summer chuckled and went back to work. "Rosie
taught me how to make flour tortillas from scratch. I'm
making breakfast tacos. Do you like them?"

"I don't know. I like how Rosie makes tacos."

Travis finally came to his senses and went to the stove.
"You'll like how Summer does it, too. I'll bet they're good.
Now, go wash up. All the way to the elbows, please."

Jenna frowned but raced off to the bathroom down the
hall, where a step stool would allow her to easily wash
her own hands. Travis grunted his approval and turned
to the sink, using the heavy-duty soap to wash up.

"I'm making a variety of tacos, some very mild for
Jenna. Potato and egg. Egg and cheese."

He chuckled. "That kid loves peppers. Anything hot
and spicy. She can stand things with a lot more fire than
I can. It's amazing."

"Oh, okay. Well, I'll set out jalapenos and she can add
them if she likes. If you're ready to sit, I'm ready to serve."

Suddenly Travis didn't want her serving their breakfast.
He wanted to serve her. He wanted to take care of her and
bring her special foods until she smiled. She didn't smile
nearly enough to suit him. But he had a feeling Summer
wouldn't have any part of that. She was too proud. Her
ego would get in the way.

At that moment Jenna dashed back into the kitchen

and dragged her chair from under the table, out where she could climb onto it. After she was seated, Travis helped shove the chair closer—just as Summer set steaming plates on the table.

"You'll be joining us, won't you?" He stared into those unique blue eyes and nearly lost himself in a tidal wave of longing.

"Um, I'm not really hungry."

"Sit," he ordered. "And have something to eat. You look like a good, strong wind would blow you away."

Summer froze where she was and scowled.

Jenna dug into her breakfast and paid no attention to the electricity snapping between the two adults in the room.

He knew Summer had to be tough in order to keep on living, after everything she'd been through. But she would soon find out he was much more determined. Setting his jaw, he went to her side and ushered her into an empty chair at the table. Then he grabbed a plate and utensils and put a place setting before her.

The last thing he did was try a smile. "There you go. Now, eat. *Please.*"

By the time he'd taken his regular seat, Summer had put a tentative spoonful of egg into a tortilla. She was so beautiful with her pride at cooking something new. Her spine was straight, her chin high.

He came to a quick decision. He didn't want to spend a moment out of her presence. The last few days had been interminable without her. Today she would be coming with him wherever he went.

"Today is our day to visit the needy in town."

Jenna ignored the comment. She was used to their monthly forays in charitable giving, but Summer looked up. "Yes, I know. Rosie and I have everything ready. I'll help you pack the car before you go."

"Thank you. But it's before *we* go. You'll be joining us."

"But I have a lot to do right here."

With one forceful shake of his head, he shot down that excuse. "It's important for Jenna that we present a united effort. Besides, I'd like for you to meet some of the towns-people." And he wanted to spend the day with her, getting to know her better.

He wasn't leaving her any wiggle room and knew she might be feeling trapped. "Tell you what," he said. "After I drop Jenna at my aunt's later, we can stop by Stockard's and check on your car. We'll kill two birds with one trip that way."

To his surprise, Summer brightened and said, "I guess it'll be all right. We can leave after we do the dishes and load the SUV."

Well, that was easy. Too easy. He had a niggling feeling she had just gotten something she'd been after all along. But for the life of him, he couldn't imagine what was going on behind those innocent-looking, wide blue eyes.

After a few hours of driving around town, Summer's head was spinning. They'd delivered a week's worth of meals to a widow and her three youngsters. Another batch of Rosie's cakes and pies went to a single father who worked from home as a carpenter. His teenage sons were glad to help and offered to take some of the desserts around to the elderly who lived in the neighborhood.

People everywhere Summer, Travis and Jenna went were overjoyed, not so much with the donations, but with Travis for remembering them. There were needy people living in Chance. But it looked as though none of them were suffering or isolated.

They dropped Jenna off at her great-aunt's house and bumped into Rosie on their way out. It seemed Travis's aunt would be assisting with the flower arrangements and clothing for the wedding. In passing, Rosie mentioned to Summer that she was definitely going to ask Jenna to take a prominent part in the wedding.

Travis heard the exchange but didn't have much to say until they were alone, back in the SUV and on their way to the mechanic's garage. "I'm not sure if Jenna should become that involved in the wedding. I don't want her getting any more hurt by Rosie's leaving than she is already."

He turned his head. "Was it your idea?"

"Yes. But I think if Jenna becomes more involved with the wedding plans, it might be easier for her to envision Rosie leaving. If she's having a problem with Rosie going away, it could be partly because she doesn't know where she'll be going. Um, like she doesn't know where her mother went."

A charged silence shot through the SUV, electrifying the air.

Finally, Travis cleared his throat. "Perhaps you're right. I don't believe Rosie will completely turn her back on Jenna after she leaves. Not like her mother has. The newlyweds will show up for holidays, and I'm positive Rosie would always remember to send birthday cards."

He drew a breath and swallowed. "It won't be the same situation at all."

Summer took a big risk and said what was on her mind. "Do you ever hear from Jenna's mother? Do you know where she is?"

"No. But in an emergency I could find her. I set up a

nice trust fund for my ex-wife when she left, so I wouldn't worry about how she was getting along. She can't touch the principal but spends the income. The bankers know her whereabouts."

"That was nice of you. To set that up, I mean. Uh… did your ex hurt you very much when she left?" Had she really said that? What was the matter with her?

"Never mind," she added quickly. "That's none of my business. Forget I asked."

"No, it's okay. It hurt that I'd been so wrong about her in the beginning. But it was my fault, not hers. Callie was never cut out to be a good mother and, if I'd been a little less pushy, I would have seen that about her all along."

Summer didn't know what to say. Maybe it would be better to stay silent.

She looked up through the windshield as Travis prepared to turn into Stockard's parking lot. At first her mind was still involved in what they'd been discussing, and she blindly stared out without really seeing what was right in front of her.

Then she did. The same white pickup! She'd been looking for it all morning. And there it was, turning out of the Feed and Seed Store across the highway from the mechanic's shop.

"Oh!" The exclamation was out of her mouth before she'd thought about it.

"What? What's the matter?" Travis stepped on the brake.

Silently, she glared at the man in the pickup, trying to assure herself he was really *the one*.

The man she knew as Bobby was driving this time and glanced up, getting a look at her face, before turning down the highway in the other direction. He'd seen her—must have. Oh, no.

"Summer, are you all right? What's wrong?" Travis completed his turn into Stockard's yard.

"Did you see that truck? Do you know the owner?"

"What truck?"

"The one that just passed us. The white one with the writing on the side in red."

"No, sorry. But there're probably several people who own trucks like that around Chance. Why?"

Now she'd done it. What was she going to say? "I just thought the man driving looked like someone I know. But..."

Travis shook his head as he put the SUV in park. "You'd better not go around saying things like that in public. How likely is it that you would recognize anyone in Chance, Texas, when you haven't ever been here before? It's a small town, and people gossip, Summer. And the gossip isn't always based on reality. I expect they're already talking about you showing up with no family or friends in a town like Chance that's so far off the main roads. I don't really care what they say, but I doubt you want anyone to start hinting that you're a little eccentric or crazy, do you?"

Chapter 6

Summer was still shaking from the silent confrontation of gazes with a man she hadn't faced in five years. *Her quarry.* The criminal who hadn't yet seen justice for his crimes.

A P.I. she'd hired back home had said this second man had changed his name—several times. That's why it had taken so long to run him down. Simply asking about him by name would probably not work to uncover his whereabouts. What should she do?

"Looks like the sheriff is here," Travis remarked, as he pulled into a parking spot on the other side of the garage.

Maybe she should talk to the sheriff about the man. All along that's what she'd been planning to do when she finally found him. Turn him in to the nearest lawman and call the police back home.

But how could she do that, when she didn't have the foggiest idea what name he was using or where he lived or worked? She would sound crazy—just as Travis had said.

"Don't get too friendly with the sheriff, Summer. He's not particularly forthcoming with anyone connected to the Chance family."

"Oh? Why is that?"

Travis grimaced as he put his hand on the door handle. "Long story." He hesitated, his hand frozen, and turned to her instead of getting out. "My father actually brought the sheriff in from another part of the state to run for the office nearly thirty years ago. They became friends. Then, fifteen years later, this sheriff arrested Dad for the murder of my mother—even though the circumstantial evidence against him was pretty slim."

"Rosie told me none of you believe your father was guilty of the crime. Why did the jury find him guilty?"

Travis shrugged. "The best I can figure is they believed my father had the only motive. He'd been having an affair, and the prosecutor convinced everyone that my parents must've had a huge argument over it that became violent."

"But you and your family don't buy that idea?"

"Mom knew all along that Dad had other women in his life from time to time. Somehow my father didn't get the fidelity gene from his parents that the rest of the family seems to have. My mother lived with the knowledge. So, why would they argue over another woman all of a sudden? And besides, my old man would never hit a woman—especially not Mom. Despite how everything looked, I know he loved her."

Summer nodded but didn't have anything to say. What could you say about a dead man's motives?

Travis turned and stepped out of the SUV, so she unbuckled to follow him. But she had decided against mentioning anything to the sheriff about her quest to find her man. Not until she felt more positive about her identification and knew where he was staying.

The sheriff tipped his hat to them as they walked up to Jimmy. Then the sheriff simply got into his cruiser and left without a word. She noticed Travis visibly relaxing his shoulders as the sheriff drove off.

"Travis. Ms. Wheeler. Nice afternoon." Jimmy Stockard tilted his head toward them. "What can I do for you?"

What could he do for her? How about her car?

"What'd the sheriff want, Jimmy?" Travis strolled beside Jimmy back into the shade of the bay.

Summer noticed her car inside the garage, but it wasn't up on the rack.

"He was asking about Ms. Wheeler here. I was surprised when he didn't stop you to say hello."

"Me? What did he want to know about me?"

Jimmy raised his palms and shrugged. "Not much. Just your name and where you were staying. I got the impression he was simply checking on the strange car with the Connecticut plates. Wouldn't think anything of it if I were you."

Travis turned to her. "Don't worry about the sheriff. Most of the town is probably gossiping about the pretty new woman in Chance. He was just curious. You're not a criminal. Nothing for Sheriff Austin McCord to have on his radar."

Was everyone in town talking about her? What if word of her being in town got back to the man she'd been chasing? Would he run? Would he try to head her off?

It was all she could do not to wring her hands. To keep from becoming hysterical, she tried to change the subject.

"Jimmy, why aren't you working on my car? Is it too far gone to fix?"

Travis touched her shoulder and brought her attention around to him. "Meant to mention that Jimmy called me yesterday to say he'd had to order parts. And he wasn't sure how long it might take to have them shipped in."

Her mouth dropped open. "It slipped your mind?"

Travis grinned sheepishly. "Lots going on."

She closed her eyes for a second and counted to ten. "Do you need a down payment to order the parts, Jimmy?"

"No, ma'am. Travis said to put it on his order for ranch spare parts. That's good enough for the supplier and for me. After I get the parts in, I should be able to get your car back in shape in a couple of weeks. Or maybe three, depending on how backed up I am then."

Summer ignored Travis for the moment, but she was gathering up steam to tell him what she thought of his trying to have things his own way—privately. "Can you at least give me an estimate of what the work will cost?"

Jimmy threw Travis a quick glance but answered her. "Won't know for sure until we get into the job. But since you're working for Travis, I consider you good for whatever."

She nodded to Jimmy and stormed past Travis, heading back to the SUV. She didn't want his charity. It would bring her too much guilt. Despite his charitable side, her boss was the most arrogant, self-important man she'd ever met.

All the more reason not to let herself get too close to him or Jenna. Good thing she was finding out about him now, before it was too late.

Travis kept his eyes on the road but could feel the tension in the air. "I'm sorry I didn't remember to tell you about Stockard's call. I was in Austin when his call came in, and it slipped my mind."

Not totally true, of course. He'd dreaded mentioning his "arrangement" with Stockard, knowing she wouldn't take it well. He'd eased back into his old ways and had been trying to control her even though he knew she hated it. But he needed to keep her here until the two of them could explore what was going on between them. Every time she came near, his pulse spiked and his groin tightened. His mind had deliberately blocked the whole call.

"Can't we consider it an advance on your pay?" He was grasping at straws here.

"You bet we will. And I want a full accounting of every penny you spend on my behalf. I don't need your charity."

Yeah? But maybe she did—just a little. He wouldn't mention that fixing up her old, beat-up Ford would cost almost as much as if he'd simply bought her a new one— an idea that was gaining traction in his mind every minute.

"I have one more stop to make before we go back to the ranch. Okay?" What he wanted was time enough for her to cool off before they went home.

She folded her arms over her chest. "We've already given out all the food supplies. Did we forget something?"

Good. Her mind was beginning to move on to other things. He hoped to hell their next stop wouldn't seem too familiar and bring up the whole charity dispute again. But he had no choice—he was committed now.

"This man is different from all the others. He's an old classmate fallen on hard times." Travis swung the steering wheel and headed for the edge of town. "Bodie Barnes has a problem with alcohol, but it's not entirely his fault. His father was the town drunk for years. And that was particularly hard on Bodie as a kid. His old man found an opportunity to embarrass him at every football game, practice or party. None of us kids could ever go to Bodie's house after school—our parents worried his father was too unpredictable."

"Sounds like an awful way to grow up. Were you two friends?"

"More like friendly adversaries, I'd guess you'd say. I knew he had trouble at home. But whenever we competed for honors or positions, I'd still try my best to win. And I did win most of the time. I'm not proud of trying to outdo a guy who had so many problems at home, but that's all in the past."

"Nice of you to try to help him at last."

Travis winced at her tone, but he deserved her disdain. "I have tried a couple of times in the past to help him, but without much luck. After my dad went to prison and I was running the ranch, I hired his father as a wrangler so there'd be enough money to send Bodie to college. But that didn't work out."

"What happened?"

Man, this was hard to say. Why the hell had he even brought it up?

"Bodie's father came to work drunk one time too many and caused an accident that involved several of the other wranglers. One good man lost his finger in the screwup."

Travis remembered the day as if it was yesterday. "I was hot. Furious—mostly at myself for bringing him on board. Fired Bodie's dad on the spot and told him to stay off the Bar-C for good."

Holding his breath, he finished the story. "Two days later the old man hanged himself in a tree behind his house. Took a week before anyone noticed the body."

"That's terrible."

"Yes, it is. My only excuse is that I was too young to know better."

"I don't mean what you did. Getting angry probably

didn't help anything, but you were right to fire a man like that."

He felt his chest easing and began breathing again. "Range work is hard and dangerous enough as it is," he admitted. "I'd hoped the physical labor would sober him up. But he was too far hooked on drink."

Shaking his head, he managed to continue the tale of long ago. "I felt terrible about the whole thing and tried to make a deal with Bodie's college to finish paying his tuition. He wouldn't hear of it. He quit school and vowed never to come back to this town."

"But he's here now?"

"Came back about three months ago and moved into the old, abandoned place where he'd grown up. He hasn't had much luck finding a job, since he's spent some time in prison, and I hear lately he's begun drinking the same as his father."

"And he won't take your money—or your food." It wasn't a question, so Summer already seemed to understand the problem.

"No. But I've got to try one more time. I'm hoping Bodie can still be saved."

He pulled the SUV up in front of the ramshackle dump where Bodie Barnes was living. If you could call it *living*. The place didn't even have running water.

"I should have the sheriff condemn this mess," he muttered under his breath.

He was only half kidding. But he intended to get Bodie Barnes out of this place today or else burn it down.

Summer's eyes were wide as he turned the key and shut off the SUV. "Um, maybe he's living in his truck?"

"If he has any sense." Which Travis doubted.

Bodie stepped out of the shade behind the house. It was hard for Travis to tell what kind of shape he might be in.

From this distance, he could plainly see Bodie's face, but his expression gave nothing away. His eyes were glazed and he had dark circles under them. Had he been drinking? Or had he just been isolated and alone too long?

"Stay in the car," Travis cautioned her. "Let me talk to him for a few minutes."

Travis left the engine running, the air conditioner on and the windows rolled up. He didn't want Summer to hear their conversation. No telling what Bodie might say.

"Well, well," his old friend muttered as he walked closer. "If it isn't the great man himself. What are you doing on my property?"

Bodie seemed steady on his feet, and Travis prayed the man still had his senses about him at this hour of day. "I came to offer you a job on the Bar-C." He held his breath, hoping for Bodie's sake he would take the offer in the spirit in which it was offered.

Bodie closed his eyes for a second, as a pained expression streaked across his face. "You're joking, right? You want me to take my old man's job as a wrangler? Didn't that work out badly enough for you the first time?"

"Ah, come on," Travis said with a shake of his head. "All that stuff happened a long time ago, and I've regretted it every day since. I'm giving you a chance for a different kind of life. You could apprentice under one of the foremen part-time, and earn your keep doing odd jobs around the ranch for the rest of the time. I'd want you to move into one of the bunkhouses today so you could start right away. What do you say?"

Travis watched him carefully as Bodie shot a sharp glance behind him, toward the SUV.

Instead of answering the question directly, he said, "I'd heard you'd thrown out Callie a few years ago. This new one measure up to your standards better? She's prettier than Callie."

Travis held his temper. Callie was one more thing Bodie had wanted in high school that Travis had won instead. But all of their competitions, all of their old squabbles, had been over for a long time.

"She's just on the Bar-C temporarily. Acting as a housekeeper until I can locate someone permanent for the job. She's not my girlfriend."

"I saw the way you looked at her when you stepped out of the SUV. You got that serious look."

Travis did not want to have this conversation. "What about my job offer? You ready to leave this…" he waved a hand at the dump of an old house "…place? I could use the extra hand on the ranch. We've been friends a long time, bud. Let's help each other out."

To his surprise, that seemed to do the trick, as Bodie nodded his agreement. "Yeah, that'd be okay. I'll head out to the Bar-C later this evening."

Well, Travis hadn't expected much of a thank-you. But some sort of appreciation might've been nice. Shrugging off Bodie's foul attitude, he chalked the whole thing up to a grudging win and nodded, too.

"Fine. I'll tell Barrett to find a place for you. Ring him when you get to the gate." With that, he turned and walked back to the waiting SUV.

Before he could reach for the door, his cell phone rang. Jenna's name appeared on the screen.

"What's up, Jenna?"

"Come get me, Daddy. I want to go back to the ranch with you now."

He knew it was the foal she was dying to see. "You don't want to stay with Auntie June overnight?"

"Oh, *Daaaddy*. I had to stand still for *hours* while

Auntie and Rosie took measurings of me. I want to go home."

Travis stifled a chuckle at her veiled excuses for wanting to see her new filly. "All right. Summer and I will swing by in a few minutes and pick you up. Okay?"

"See you, Daddy." Jenna hung up the phone.

Opening the SUV's door, he stepped into the driver's seat, still smiling at his daughter's words while he put away the phone.

"What happened?" Summer sounded slightly frightened as she stared out the window.

When Travis looked, he found his former friend right where he'd left him, standing in front of the SUV and studying Summer through the windshield. "I offered him a job, and he took it. Don't pay any attention to him. I'm sure he'll swallow whatever is stuck in his craw as soon as he starts earning money. The past is the past."

"I hope he thinks so." But Summer didn't sound too sure.

Travis put the SUV in reverse and backed up. "Jenna just called and wants to be picked up. That'll be our last stop. Okay by you?"

"I'm ready to go back to work. There's still plenty to do at the house."

"Well, now, I was hoping you'd take the rest of the afternoon off and let me show you around the horses. Jenna would probably love to introduce you to her new filly."

"I will, if you'll take me off the clock and not pay me for the time."

Shoot. He couldn't pull anything over on her. Not even a few extra hours of pay. Giving this woman even a small bit of help was going to be a struggle from here on out. God help him.

* * *

He rounded his aunt's neighborhood street corner, while thinking about all the places on the ranch he wanted to show Summer. But they were running out of daylight, and he knew he'd never get Jenna away from her foal for long today. He would probably have to wait until Monday, when Jenna went back to school, to have a good tour around the ranch operations.

Lost in thought, he didn't see the blinking blue lights behind him until he heard a siren and glanced up. "What the…?"

"Are you speeding?"

Putting on the brakes and pulling over, he said, "No. I'm not speeding. I don't know what this is about." He stopped and shut off the motor. "Stay in the car. I shouldn't be too long."

As he opened the door and got out, a sheriff's deputy's white pickup came to a stop behind him. But it was the sheriff himself who stepped out. McCord had been driving his personal cruiser when they'd seen him at Stockard's earlier. Travis wondered about the change and why he'd been stopped.

"What's the problem, Sheriff?"

"Wanted a word with you, Chance." The sheriff hiked up his waistband, put his hands on his hips and stood about a foot away.

"You could've called the ranch." Being stopped by the side of the road didn't make Travis all that eager to stand around chatting with the sheriff.

McCord ignored the dig, spread his feet and tried to throw back his shoulders. At the age of sixty, the sheriff's body had seen better days. He hadn't exactly taken care of himself over the years, especially in the last few years since his wife had died. And the man's protruding belly kept getting in the way of his best attempts at standing tall.

The sheriff glared at him through dark sunglasses. "Saw you heading toward June's. Thought I'd save the call."

As the years had gone by, Sheriff McCord had become less and less friendly with the Chance family—especially Travis. But he still showed up on Bar-C land at the drop of a hat. Whenever he wanted to arrest one of the wranglers for a bad Saturday night on the town, or when he needed to speak to Travis about county road right-of-ways, or for just about any reason he could manufacture.

Travis didn't care for the idea of the sheriff wandering alone on Bar-C property without warning Travis in advance. But there wasn't much he could do about it. His father had given the sheriff free trespassing rights when he'd first hired him thirty years ago, and Travis hadn't been able to find a good way around those rights since.

Maybe he should try giving McCord a break. The sheriff hadn't abused his position. Or, at least, he hadn't yet. Just lately, though, it seemed the sheriff had developed some kind of chip on his shoulder. Travis wondered about the man's personal life since his wife's death.

"What did you want?" That was the best he could do while standing in the middle of the street.

"Wanted to ask about the woman you've taken in." The sheriff opened a small notepad, a reminder of his old-school ways. "According to Stockard, her name is Summer Wheeler and she's just passing through. That right?"

What on earth did McCord want with Summer? "That's right. Why?"

"I'm running her plates to see if the car was stolen.

Just thought I'd mention that. What do you know about her background?"

Travis had no intention of telling the sheriff what his brother had learned. He intended to stick with Summer's version of the story.

"She said she was traveling around Texas, looking for a place to settle down. Her car broke down right outside town, and now she's stuck here until Stockard can get the parts in. She needed a temporary job to carry her through, and I had something she could do. That's about it."

"Don't you think it's kind of odd she was passing through Chance? This place ain't on the road to anywhere."

"Ah, look, Sheriff, if you have a lot of questions, why don't you ask her to come in and talk?" Not that he would rush her down to the sheriff's office anytime soon for such an interrogation.

The sheriff had no business snooping into a private citizen's background. Texans respected independent spirits—they didn't persecute them.

"Think I'll make a few calls first, Chance. And if I were you, I'd watch my back around her. Something don't feel right about her story. She could be dangerous."

Oh, for pity's sake. "If that's all that's on your mind, McCord— I'm late to pick up my daughter. You know where to find us." He turned and strode to the driver's side door.

"Mark my words, Chance," the sheriff called out to his back. "This one will be trouble."

Chapter 7

An angry man, lost in the shadows of a cottonwood tree, watched as Travis drove Summer and Jenna down the side streets at the edge of town, heading back to the Bar-C.

Odd how that bastard, Travis Chance, had hooked up with such a screwed-up broad, he thought. Hard to imagine the high and mighty CEO of the Bar-C with a woman the likes of her. They seemed to come from different planets.

Maybe linking the two of them together would be just the break he'd been looking for. After all, the Bar-C was ripe with opportunities to make Travis Chance worry and wonder what was coming next. Yes, indeed. Any ranch would be chock-full of potential dangers and numerous ways to make a point. And he certainly had a point he wanted to drive home.

Whistling as the Bar-C SUV drove out of sight, he hustled back to his truck. There were lots of plans to make and not much time left.

His mind whirled with possibilities. Yes, sirree. Now he could solve a couple of his biggest problems with one set of plans. Laughing for the first time in what seemed like years, he stepped up into the pickup, as endless images ran through his mind. Images of maneuvers guaranteed to cause fear and anguish.

Payback. At long last.

This was sure going to be fun.

Chapter 8

Summer lived through the rest of the weekend—barely. Without Rosie to rely on, she'd had to think up various ways of encouraging Jenna to eat after she refused to leave the barn. Travis had made up a bed of blankets for his daughter so she could stay with her new horse. The whole weekend had been a tricky balancing act and tried Summer's creativity, along with her patience.

But by Sunday night, she found herself fighting an attraction to both Jenna and her father even though she hadn't seen a lot of either one of them. Jenna seemed so lost, so hungry for attention. And Travis—Travis was really getting under her skin. Her first impression of him as the sexiest man she'd ever met still held true. Every time he came near she got goose bumps. It wasn't right and she didn't want to have these feelings, but there it was. She kept trying to push them aside and kept reminding herself that he was kind but controlling and would be impossible to live with for long. He was her boss and the closer she got to him the more she felt guilty about keeping her secrets.

Monday morning dawned fresh and new, with the sky decked out in crisp, clear sunshine and the day full of glowing potential. A Texas sort of Monday, according to Travis.

Rosie was back to work at the ranch and asked her to drive Jenna to school. Summer was pleased to cooperate and hoped that the time spent alone with the little girl would do them both some good.

But Jenna was sullen, silent and grumpy on the way into town. Every word the little girl uttered made it quite clear that she believed her life had become a terrible ordeal. Seemed little Jenna would much rather stay in the barn with her horse than be forced to go to school.

Summer had to laugh inside, thinking of how at that age she too had wanted to do other things besides go to school. But she wouldn't dare let Jenna catch her smiling. So she smothered every chuckle and tried to be as sympathetic yet firm as she knew how.

After she dropped Jenna off, Summer took a slow drive around town on the way home. Checking everywhere, every store and every side street, she hoped to locate the truck and the man she'd now seen twice.

If she got lucky, she could at least jot down the license number and the sign on the truck's door panel. Then she would find someone to tell her where the truck belonged. The truck was the key—even if checking on it meant she would need to call on the P.I. back home for help.

But she wasn't lucky. Not today. Giving up temporarily, she headed back to the Bar-C, ready to begin her day.

Travis met the SUV as she drove into the side yard of the ranch house. He waved and came her way, looking so energetic and full of good spirit that her mouth actually watered.

Smiling, he stepped beside her door and waited until she turned off the engine. When she reached for the door handle and turned her gaze in his direction, a sharp, sudden hunger leapt into his eyes. She felt it to the tips of her toes.

Her body's automatic response caused a war to erupt inside her. She wanted this man. This beautiful but decidedly arrogant man who was currently her boss. But wanting him the way she did seemed totally illogical. She *couldn't.*

But she did want him. No getting around it.

However, wanting—even desperate wanting—didn't necessarily mean she would have to act on the urges. Lots of people lived with unrequited desire. But her throat went dry at the idea of never having a chance to taste those lips, of never having those muscular arms hold her during the heat of passion.

Sighing, she wondered why her life had turned out this way. If life was fair, then why couldn't she have him? And also have everything he represented: honor, trust, protection, love?

Wow. Flights of fancy? Not her usual style, and they weren't going to get her anywhere. She must remember he was far above and beyond her reach. All she could have where Travis was concerned were daydreams.

No choice but to find some way of moving past her raging hormones. The idea of the two of them together seemed ludicrous when she considered it. He was the well-respected owner of a gigantic working ranch. She was the penniless widow of a mob boss's son. The disinherited daughter of snobby parents who refused to acknowledge her existence. Almost laughable.

Travis performed selfless works of charity. The towns-people cared about him, and he had a loving family. She was nothing but a selfish liar without one single soul who gave a damn whether she lived or died.

No, when she thought of it that way, the two of them didn't seem like a particularly suitable pairing. In fact, they were completely unsuitable.

Still, as he opened the door for her and his back muscles rippled under his shirt with the effort, she felt her chest constrict. Breathing became difficult.

He reached for her hand and helped her climb out of the SUV. The simple touch of his hand to hers caused an electric tingle she'd never felt in her entire life. It moved all the way up to her shoulder.

Puzzled by the sudden, intense physical reaction, she quickly withdrew her hand and looked away. Ever since the tragedy and her hospitalization, and after finding out the truth about her husband's family, her sex drive had nose-dived to near zero on the heat meter.

And now was when her body chose to rebound? With a man who could control the success or failure of her life's goal?

She chanced a quick glance into his eyes. Travis met her gaze, and a flash of awareness told her he'd felt the sizzle, too.

Folding her arms over her chest, she broke the connection, turned her back and headed toward the house.

"Whoa. What did I do?" He came up behind her and put his arm on her shoulder.

"Nothing." The spot where he'd laid his hand tingled and heated, but she didn't turn.

"Haven't you forgiven me for the Stockard deal yet?"

That spun her around and away from his touch. "There's nothing to forgive. You did what you thought best. Besides, you're my boss—my forgiveness isn't important."

Travis looked confused. "Of course it is. Everything about you is important."

"Don't say that." She wanted to walk away but couldn't seem to force her feet to move. "I have to go. There's work to do."

"Wait." He reached out a hand as if to stop her, but she hadn't moved a muscle. "I thought we could… That is… I planned on you taking the day off. You worked all weekend and, since Rosie has returned now, today should be your weekend."

"There's nothing for me to do. I'd rather work."

He drew his hand back to his side but left the silly grin plastered on his face. "I have something for you to consider doing on your day off. I've been wanting to get to know you better. Just the two of us. Come with me and I'll show you around the ranch. It's a big operation with many different things going on. I need to check on some projects, and I'd hoped you come along."

Tempted, she studied him for a moment. His green eyes glimmered in the warm sunlight. His big, megawatt smile silently begged her to see it his way and accompany him. But she knew he was really just controlling things again.

"All right. Let me just check with Rosie." Damn. This was a very bad idea.

"I'll tag along," he said in a voice filled with good humor. "I asked her to make up a couple of picnic lunches for the trail. We can pick them up on the way to the barn."

"The trail?" Uh-oh. All of a sudden her mind filled with dread, along with a ton of reasons for why she couldn't go. She'd been right. Bad idea.

"Sure." He looped her arm around his in a move that screamed he would not let her change her mind at this point. "The first part of our tour needs to be made on horseback. Then, this afternoon, we'll switch over to the helicopter. It'll be a great day. You're going to love it."

Fifteen minutes later Travis was still praying he was right and had not just been giving voice to his fervent wishes. Summer would love seeing the ranch. She would.

She was different. Different from any woman he'd ever known. And certainly much different from Callie.

Callie would've hated riding around on horseback, touring the ranch and seeing some of his big accomplishments. He'd never even bothered to invite his ex-wife, knowing how she preferred shopping and visiting with friends over riding and ranch business. They'd had little in common throughout their marriage, and they'd never really done anything as a solid couple—except produce the most beautiful baby girl in the world.

And even that Callie had walked away from in the end.

With some surprise, Travis noted how the sting of his ex-wife's rejection no longer bothered him the way it once had. Searching his conscious mind, he couldn't find any remnants of the pain he'd felt when Callie left without so much as a backward glance.

He'd finally come around to accepting the end of his marriage. About time. But more than that, he'd realized that the end could've been predicted from the very beginning. And avoided. But only if he'd stopped acting like a general on a campaign long enough to listen to the woman he'd thought he loved.

Callie, even at her tender age, had probably known the truth from the very start. But they'd been friends and she'd liked him, liked him a lot, and hadn't known how to make him see the truth without hurting them both. So, she'd gone along—swept away on the tide of his arrogance.

She'd been too young then to understand how much worse things would be for everyone if she waited to leave until they'd had a child and made a home together. And unfortunately, that's exactly what she'd done in the end.

Not entirely Callie's fault, he reminded himself.

Glancing at Summer as she gathered up their picnic lunch, he vowed not to make the same mistakes with her. He could be pushy and overbearing sometimes. Well, most of the time, he supposed. That's exactly why he knew he could never marry again. He would not subject another woman to his arrogance or to living the kind of isolated ranch life that he thrived on.

He'd been luckier with Jenna. His little girl loved the ranch. Loved the life they had. Though she hadn't been given any choice in the matter. But he'd made a promise to himself that, when the time came, he would send her off to a fancy school. Someplace that could teach her all the things that mattered to a woman. All the things she didn't have access to on the Bar-C.

It would kill him if Jenna never came back to the ranch after that. But he would have to accept it as the way things were meant to be. Over the years, he'd become good at accepting the ways the world worked.

Glancing over at Summer, his brain told him that here was a woman who would leave him, too, in the end. He should walk away. Steel his heart. But every time he looked at her, his heart stuttered and his gut churned. He had never wanted anyone so much. Maybe he was in for a big hurt in the end, but he was bound to take this as far as he could. He was no coward.

"All set to go, boss?" Summer looked up at him with a mixture of trepidation and readiness shining in her eyes.

Stopping in midstride, he fought his own natural tendencies to push and tried to be fair. "Are you sure you want to go through with this? Maybe a day at the movies or reading a book would be more to your liking for your day off."

"No. This will be fine. I want to know all about the Bar-C. I'd like to understand what you're saying when you and Jenna talk about ranch things."

Her deep blue eyes were stormy, and his pulse jumped at the sight. Blood surged through his veins, torturing him with sudden images of the two of them alone. He desperately needed to see that same, intense look in her eyes, slightly glazed and dark with passion, as the two of them made love.

The idea took his breath away. Gasping for air, he shook off the images, scolding his libido for turning up the heat at the most inappropriate times. Summer would be touring the ranch with him today only because she felt obligated to do so for her job.

Deep in his gut he knew the truth, even though he tried to deny it. Summer, like his ex-wife, would be heading off for one of Texas's big cities as soon as her car was fixed. She wasn't really that different.

But for today, he would take her any way he could get her. Even if only because she felt obligated, if that meant he could spend the day with her alone. He just needed to remember not to take advantage of her vulnerability.

She *was* up to this. She had to be. Just because her knees shook at the thought of riding a horse—of potentially losing control to another being with a mind of its own—didn't mean she shouldn't try it anyway. Life was filled with difficult adventures. Riding a horse should be one of the least treacherous trials she had to face.

"Have you ever ridden?" Travis moved into the corral,

where one of his ranch hands had left two horses, already saddled and with picnic baskets, ready to go.

"Horses? Um, a long time ago." She stood stock-still so he wouldn't see her shaking and tried to steady her nerves.

"How long?"

"I was ten. My mother decided a perfectly schooled woman should know how to ride in English style."

"Western riding is a lot different. We'll broaden your schooling." He moved to the left side of one of the horses and fiddled with the reins.

Both of the horses sidestepped, turned their faces to sneer at whoever was bothering them, and then flipped their tails.

Scared, Summer tried to put the worst possible scenarios out of her mind. The horse wouldn't take off while under her. She wouldn't fall off and break her neck. She would be perfectly capable of controlling such a huge creature. Biting her lip, she waited for Travis to tell her what to do next.

When he seemed satisfied with the tack, he turned to her. His expression changed from expectant to uncertain. "You look terrified. If you'd rather not do this, we can use the ATVs. They're loud and scare the herds, but if you'd be more comfortable…"

"No. I'll do it. One of my psychologists said I should deliberately put myself in situations that stretch my comfort zones. It's the only way to really make progress."

"One of your psychologists? How many do you have?"

Oh, shoot. She hadn't meant to say that. He would believe she was crazy for real now.

Trying to backpedal and make light of it, she said, "I think I told you that right after…uh…the tragedy, I had sort of a breakdown. It took a few months and lots of doctors to make me well again." Not that she thought she would ever be completely well.

The only thing that might make a real difference to her mental health would be seeing the man she'd been hunting, a man nicknamed Hoss, get what he deserved. Summer hoped finding him and making him face his justice wouldn't take too much longer.

"Uh-huh. Are you sure about riding today, sugar?" Travis's expressive eyes filled with concern for her needs.

But that wasn't what she wanted for him. Not at all. Travis was too good to become involved in her dismal past. Or in her iffy future, for that matter. Her problems were her problems. She wanted him to have a nice day, as he'd planned. Somehow she would have to keep him, along with her own unruly mind, firmly rooted in the right now.

"I'm sure." She forced a smile but wasn't positive she was pulling it off. "How do I climb aboard this beast?"

The smile or the words made Travis's face break out in his usual grin. "By not overthinking it," he said through a chuckle.

Beckoning her closer, he showed her how to grip both the reins and the horn of the saddle at the same time. "Face the horse and put your left foot in the stirrup here. Then swing your right leg up and over the horse's back. Stay fluid and try it in one smooth move. I'll help."

She did it the way he instructed but definitely not in a smooth move. Yet somehow, in seconds, she was on the back of the horse. She wanted to cry.

"Great! You look like you belong in a saddle."

He gave her a few minutes of instruction on how to sit and how to "steer," for lack of a better word. Then he mounted the other horse and demonstrated by doing the moves himself.

Some of the instructions seemed vaguely reminiscent of her earlier riding classes. But she had never before felt anything quite like sitting astride an animal this big and powerful. It was a terrifying, yet not totally unpleasant, sensation. She sensed she had far more control than she'd ever had when riding English-style as a kid.

"How are you doing? Ready to try a walk around the corral?"

"I think I've got the idea. Might as well get a head start on whatever you wanted me to see."

Travis nodded, lifted his hat and set it back down lower on his forehead. He'd insisted she wear a hat too, to keep the sun off her face, so she mimicked his moves and settled into the saddle.

"We'll take it slow and won't ride far today. You might find you like being on horseback, and we'll do it again another time."

Grimacing, she hoped he took her facial expression as another smile. If she lived through this experience, it remained to be seen whether she would still be around for another time.

She wasn't sure how much longer she could keep lying to him. She needed to find her man and move on.

Travis kept a tight rein on his stallion and made sure Summer's mare stayed docilely in line beside them. He'd deliberately put Summer on one of the gentlest mares in the household herd.

They stayed to the ancient horse trails, keeping a slower pace while he pointed out one of the cattle herds and then a smaller herd of sheep in the next pasture over. The necessary chore of opening and closing each gate as they rode through reminded him of his grandfather's irritation at having to put up fences at all. It had been years ago when

the Bar-C diversified their herds and added the sheep and
goats to their many varieties of cattle. Even to this day,
fences were a pain in the neck for cattle ranchers. The
Bar-C spent almost as much time and money repairing
and replacing fence as they did branding and marking the
herds in the spring.

He kept his eye out for the fence-repair teams and was
gratified to see several crews hard at work in the distance.
Riding the closer-in fence lines, looking for new breaks
or downed wire, was one of the chores he'd promised his
foreman he would accomplish today.

"What're all those buildings in the distance?" Summer
lifted her chin in the direction of the barns and sheds but
kept her fingers wrapped tightly in the reins.

"That's our quarter-horse breeding operation. My older
brother, Sam, is in charge of that division of the Bar-C.
See the two-story home off to the right? That's the house
where we grew up. My brother and his wife and son live
there now."

Travis sat back in the saddle and gazed at the place,
lost in a flash of memories centered on his carefree youth.

"Are we going to stop there?"

"Not today. Sam and Grace are in Houston at a horse-
breeders' convention. But you'll like my sister-in-law
when you meet her. She's originally from Los Angeles."

And Travis had been pleasantly surprised when Grace
took so easily to the isolated life on the ranch. "It turns
out she makes a great partner for Sam in the horse business. And on top of that, she's a terrific mother to their
son. Sam's a lucky man. My Jenna just adores Grace and
their baby."

Summer's face sobered as they walked their horses past
the old homestead. The words of pride had just popped
out of his mouth without thinking it through. But maybe

he should've figured she would be a little touchy hearing talk about babies.

But, hell, it was almost impossible to stop talking about kids if you came from Chance. They grew almost as many children here as they did heads of cattle.

After another fifteen minutes of riding, they arrived at the spot where he'd planned to set up their picnic lunch. "Here we go. We'll stop at the stock pond under that stand of trees up ahead. After lunch we need to pick a bag of pecans for Rosie. She needs them for the pies she plans to make for her reception."

."These are pecan trees?" Wide-eyed, she glanced up into the branches above their heads.

"Some of them. And a few cottonwoods and willows."

He pulled their horses to a stop over a patch of grasses and dismounted. "Let me ground the horses first, and then off you go. I'll need your help carrying the lunch packs."

It took a few seconds for her to pry the reins from her fingers. Chuckling softly at how ill at ease she still seemed on the back of the horse, he figured she would settle down after lunch. It took another minute with the horses before he turned back, expecting to find her standing on the ground. Looking up through dappled sun, he was shocked to see her still sitting astride the saddle.

"Problem?"

"How…how do you get off?"

"Same way you got on. Plant your foot in the stirrup and swing the other leg over."

"It's a long way down." She looked stiff with fear.

"Here, I'll help you off this first time. Take your feet out of the stirrups." He reached up and hooked an arm around her waist as he would've done for Jenna.

Pulling her toward him, he felt her whole body stiffen. "Relax. Let me do the work."

The breath puffed from her mouth as her body went limp. He dragged her out of the saddle and into his arms. It took some finagling to wrench her feet away from the tangle of stirrups, and her hat went flying, but in a few minutes she was clinging to him and seemed unharmed.

Wrapped in his arms, her heart beat wildly against his chest, while both of them tried to regulate their breathing. Feeling her tremble, he gazed down into her upturned face. What he saw took him completely by surprise. A thundering awareness pulsed through his veins as he saw her eyes fill with what had to be the same anticipation he felt.

His body went on alert. The whole world came down to just the two of them.

Chapter 9

Travis's heart stuttered as she laid a gentle hand against his chest. Those same electric tingles he'd been fighting for days shot straight to his gut, leaving him shaken. Overjoyed at finally having her in his arms, he wanted to shout. Still, he managed to remain silent and strong and keep the connection their eyes had made. To her credit, Summer never looked away either.

Her palm felt warm next to his skin, even through his shirt. As the breeze blew a strand of her ash-blond hair out of place, his fingers itched to touch her. He couldn't help himself, so he tucked the wayward strand behind her ear. Her breath hitched when his hand lingered against her cheek. Blinking wildly, her gaze dropped to his mouth. She looked like a woman who was thinking about being kissed.

Lowering his head to accommodate her, but not wanting to scare her by moving too fast, he slowly narrowed the gap between them. At the same time, he loosened his grip around her waist, intending to reach up and lift her chin into position for a thorough kiss.

Then suddenly, she just disappeared. One second they were chest to chest, stomach to stomach, and the next he was grasping at nothing but air.

"Ahhh," she cried as she slid down his body and landed in a heap in the dirt. "What's going on? My knees gave out."

Dang. Her first time on horseback in years. Of course her legs would be wobbly when she first dismounted. He should've thought of that. He should've thought—period.

Scooping her up, he carried her under the trees to the little shelter he and his brother Sam had built as teens. It was a place in the shade perfect for a picnic. After gently setting her down, he felt bereft without her in his arms and kicked himself for being an unthinking ass. He swore to maintain a respectable distance from now on.

However, despite clearing the fog of lust from his brain, his body still wasn't behaving with anything close to respect. No, it was something else entirely that had made him hard and hot. Shoot, he needed to dig up a lot of his famous control. And fast.

He'd been about to kiss her.

Summer's heart still thundered in her chest as he walked away to get her a bottle of water. She'd wanted that kiss. More than she should have. Her face felt on fire as she thought of the ultimate embarrassment of collapsing at his feet.

"Here you go." Travis handed her a cold bottle, which she accepted gratefully. "That shaky feeling will stop in a moment. Happens to everyone their first time on horseback. You may have to hang on to something in order to walk. Just till the world stops rocking and rolling."

"How about if I just sit right here for a few more minutes?"

He tilted his head and smiled. "Yes, ma'am. I'll start hauling the picnic basket and drinks over."

Turning toward the horses, he hesitated, then turned back. "I think I owe you an apology."

"For what? You didn't do anything." She knew he was talking about their almost kiss but hoped he would let it pass, so her embarrassment could blow away with the breeze.

"But I almost did." Nope. He wasn't going to give it a rest. "I didn't mean to embarrass you. That was a huge loss of control on my part."

Her face grew even warmer. She had to say something to cool herself down. "Control is really important to you, isn't it?"

He looked a little confused for a second, but that soon disappeared and Travis the boss was back. "Yep, I guess it is. I have a lot of responsibilities to family and the ranch, and someone needs to look like he knows what he's doing."

Summer thought his need for control ran a lot deeper than that, but she wouldn't challenge him on it. He was her boss, after all.

Instead, she decided to play a little verbal volleyball and change the subject. "I can't help wondering what you're like when you just let go," she said with what she hoped was a come-hither look.

This time the flush went up Travis's neck. His eyes took on that deep evergreen color they always got whenever he was secretly looking at her with the desire she knew he must be feeling. That look of his always did it for her. And it did it this time, too. She felt those zinging impulses down deep again. Stirring her insides and making her wish for something he obviously didn't want to happen. If he'd wanted her, why hadn't he kissed her yet?

"I don't *just let go*. That has never worked out for me."

"Never?"

He laughed and shook his head. "Why should I? I like my life fine the way it is."

Summer didn't think much of his personal life. After all, his wife had left him, and his daughter didn't act like such an exuberantly happy child. But she wasn't about to mention anything. She'd already pushed too much. It was a pleasant morning, and she had no intention of ruining it for him by pissing him off.

"The shakes are better now," she said as she slid off the table and tested her balance. "And I'm getting hungry. Let me help you spread out the lunch."

"Are you sure you want to ride back?" Travis looked dubious while he secured the last of the coolers. "I could call for one of the hands to pick us up in a Jeep."

They'd just finished packing the picnic baskets and coolers, and Summer had mentioned she wanted a lift up to the saddle. It was late and time to leave.

But not by Jeep. "Didn't anyone ever tell you that you need to get right back up or you never will?"

"I thought that was for bicycles. And you didn't fall off. You're only a little shaky."

She rolled her eyes. "The old saying is meant for horses, too. And I'll be fine. I liked riding. It was the wobbly part afterward that didn't impress me. But I assume that gets better the more times you ride." The man wanted to control this situation, as he did all the others on the ranch, but it was her decision.

"Yeah, maybe. If you're sure."

"Help me up." Lifting her left foot and guiding it into the stirrup, she found she couldn't quite reach the saddle horn from this position.

Muttering under his breath, Travis's big hands spanned her waist and hoisted her in the air, while she swung her right leg over. "Hope you know what you're doing."

She scowled and looked down at him. "Am I in any danger by riding back with you?"

"No. But you're going to be real sore tomorrow."

Already feeling the tightness in muscles she never used, Summer scoffed. "I suspect a hot bath and some muscle cream will be all I need. Are you coming?"

Travis practically pole-vaulted around the picnic basket and into the saddle before picking up the reins. "Let's go."

She lifted her chin and tried to keep her seat the way he'd shown her before they'd started off. Now that she felt more in control of her horse, she was really beginning to enjoy the day.

After she completed her search for her quarry and left the Bar-C, when would she ever have an opportunity to ride on horseback again? The thought was depressing, but she refused to let it bring her down on such a lovely day.

She wanted to find her man, true, but she'd now also decided that she wanted a little more time on the Bar-C. Time enough to learn how things on the ranch worked. And perhaps enough time to get through to Jenna. With a quick glance at Travis—and the way the sunshine brought out the green in his eyes even with the Stetson shading half his forehead—she realized she wanted to spend more time learning about him, too.

For one thing, she'd decided she needed to find out

what kind of kisser he was. And how he would be in bed. She'd be willing to bet he was a master at pleasing a woman. The fact that his wife had left him made no difference. Summer felt positive it hadn't been due to a lack of finesse in bed on his part. Every time he'd touched her so far, he'd set off sparks.

But his treatment of her had also been rather hot and cold. Such as earlier today, when he'd come close to kissing her before she'd fallen at his feet and he'd backed off. After that, his whole demeanor changed and he'd been the boss again. Maybe she shouldn't be setting her hopes too high.

Dragging her gaze away, she looked out over the fields of grass, toward the herd grazing in the distance. What a picture this place made. He was lucky to belong here. She'd give a lot to belong someplace as special as this.

That's when it hit her. She didn't belong anywhere. With a sinking feeling, she knew with certainty that, no matter what, she would never go back to where she'd come from. Too many bad memories and people she would rather forget.

It was scary imagining not having a place to call home. Blinking back her new fears of forever facing life alone, she tried to banish thoughts of a bleak future. She needed to bury them, along with any hurtful thoughts of her old home and the many bad things that had taken place there. She didn't care to think about any of that. Not on such a wonderful day as this.

Today was all about learning ranch life and enjoying the company of a man who intrigued her. And for having the opportunity to breathe in a little unpolluted air. And scent the blowing grasses on the wind. Earthy, sensual smells kicked up by the horses' hooves.

Unfortunately, when she lifted her head and took a

deep breath, she found the early-afternoon breeze had suddenly stilled. "Can we go a little faster?" she asked when his horse came alongside her.

She needed to stir the air around her. To let the breezes clear the cobwebs and memories.

"All right. But take it easy on your first time out."

Yeah, yeah. He thought she wasn't capable of handling the horse. But she and the mare had come a long way so far today. And she wanted air.

As he was giving her instruction on how to keep the horse under control at an even faster pace, she nudged her sweet mare in the flanks and whispered, "Giddyup."

A little surprised at being asked to move faster, the mare raised her head and jolted ahead. Smiling inside at the idea of the mare becoming her new best friend, Summer reveled in the freedom of being on horseback. Riding a horse was so much more exhilarating than driving a car.

"Keep her under control," Travis warned when he caught up. "Tighten up on the reins."

Summer didn't want to listen to him. Didn't want to be cautious. She'd learned the hard way that all the caution in the world didn't mean a thing when bad times came. She'd been overly cautious with her baby. Had read the how-to books and listened to every piece of advice from the doctors. She'd done every mothering thing right. And still her little girl had died.

Taking a deep breath, Summer fought to banish the past and tried to stay solidly in the here and now. The breeze tugged at the brim of her hat, but she didn't care. The faster she went, the better. She felt alive for the first time in a long time.

Riding was intense. Freeing. It was something she could do well. She loved the exhilaration it provided.

* * *

Travis began to worry about Summer losing her focus. Riding took concentration. She'd stopped listening to him and seemed lost in her own thoughts. Never a good idea on the back of a horse.

Earlier this afternoon she'd made a crack about his need to control everything. He'd been forced to admit it was probably true. But control might mean the difference between life and death on a ranch—especially around the stock. A cowboy needed to keep his head, or things could go very wrong very fast.

He hung back and watched with concern as her mare went from a leisurely walk to a brisk walk and right into a trot. Not good. A rapid-fire trot had been known to loosen all the teeth in a cowboy's mouth. In a true trot, a horse will lift her front and back feet on opposite sides at the same time, making an unsuspecting cowboy's family jewels bounce hard against the saddle and hurt like a son-of-a-gun. The wranglers he knew all did their damnedest to keep their mounts away from any kind of trot. And though there weren't any family jewels on Summer's anatomy, trotting with her horse would still make her hurt in her most tender of spots.

Her horse pulled farther ahead, and he was treated to the sight of Summer's thick, blond hair under her hat, trailing halfway down her back and bouncing against her shoulders. For a second he lost focus too and wished he was close enough to run his fingers through all that heavenly silk.

But the sounds of clattering hooves rang in his ears and stirred him to remember the danger. "Hang on to the saddle horn and stand up in the stirrups," he yelled after her.

"What?"

"Pull your mare up!" He needed to talk to her. Explain the dangers.

She didn't tug on the reins but swiveled in the saddle to hear him better. The next few moments went by as if in terrifying slow motion. He watched with horror as the cinches on her saddle straps slipped, sending saddle and blankets, the whole works, sliding down the horse's flank in the opposite direction to her body.

He'd deliberately put her on a docile mare. A horse that didn't spook easily. But no horse could be expected to stay steady as every piece of equipment on its back began to jostle, sliding askew.

"Summer!"

Feeling totally helpless, he watched as the mare thrashed her head around and slowed to a stop. Pawing the ground, the horse tried to shake the saddle all the way off. Summer, still turned half-backward on the sliding saddle, had a panicked look on her face that had him urging his stallion to her side. He had to do something fast or the next move could be fatal.

Trying her best to hang on, Summer saw Travis's horse coming up fast. He would save her. Maybe he could pull her off the mare's back before she fell. She'd seen tricks like that done on TV.

But in the next instant, she knew it was too late for any last-minute heroics. The mare bucked, and Summer's feet slipped out of the stirrups as her bottom lost the seat altogether. Unbalanced, she felt gravity taking over.

When she hit the ground, the air was knocked right out of her lungs. Gasping for breath, she felt numb and nearing hysteria. She couldn't move or breathe and felt the ground vibrating with hoofbeats. The mare still danced and pawed right beside her head. Ohmygod, she was going to die.

Covering her head with her arms as though that would save her, she blindly listened to the hoof steps next to her ears. Paralyzed with fear, even as she caught her breath, she didn't dare try to roll out of the way.

Her numbed and terrified mind apparently didn't want to stay in the moment but shifted her right back in time to *that* night. That horrible night when she'd been locked in her basement; blindfolded, tied to the furnace and forced to listen to footsteps coming from the floors above. Sounds of terror in the darkness.

When would they come to kill her? What were they doing to her baby? How could she get free?

Suddenly, the scuffling noises around her stopped and all was quite again. Her conscious mind was dumped back into the present with a thud, but she still couldn't feel a thing. Was she alive or had she died?

"Summer!" Travis's voice broke through to her. It was like a gunshot blasting through the fog of her dread.

She didn't cry out, but a violent shudder racked her body. She was alive. Not a prisoner anymore. But she wasn't really free either. She'd become a prisoner to her nightmares.

"Are you hurt?" Travis cupped both her shoulders and lifted her to a sitting position in the dirt. "Is anything broken?"

She swallowed hard. *Breathe.*

He spent a moment checking for broken bones before pulling her all the way up to stand in his embrace. "Talk to me. Where does it hurt?"

Now that she was out of the immediate danger, all her senses had become acute. She felt every inch of his hard body pressed against hers. Heard his heavy breathing next to her ear. Could even swear she felt his heart beating in a staccato rhythm along with her own.

These heightened senses were making her feel reckless and alive. She wanted to feel more. Everything. Wonder what he would do if she tilted her head up and kissed him?

"I'm…I'm not sure," she mumbled into his chest. "Everything is numb."

"It's the adrenaline. Unfortunately, it'll wear off."

With sudden clarity, she realized adrenaline was probably the reason she was feeling so…needy…all of a sudden. This wasn't the same as earlier today when he'd wanted to kiss her. It was just a case of her rolling in the hormones. And he was providing a strong shoulder to keep her steady, not offering himself for some kind of seductive dance in the sunshine.

What was wrong with her, anyway? Maybe she was crazy.

Travis thought he must be going insane. He should be worried about her having internal injuries. Or checking for painful deep bruises and whiplash. Or wondering about whether she would sue him for everything he had.

But the lush, earthy-smelling woman in his arms was turning him on. He had developed an intense erection she was probably noticing right this minute. Hell. He needed to get a grip. Try reminding himself how vulnerable and frightened she must be. He bit the inside of his cheek and thought about the horses.

And then she shifted in his arms. Ever so slightly, pushing her hips against his groin.

With a deep breath, he fought to distract himself. Wanted to set her away, double-check her injuries and call for help. But he couldn't force himself to step back.

The thin thread of his resolution finally snapped when she tipped her head back and gazed up at him, her eyes filled with intense desire. Damn. Everything he'd wanted since the first time he'd seen her was right there, waiting for him to make the first move. So much for chivalry. So much for thinking things through.

However, it turned out he didn't make that first move. She did. She flung her arms around his neck and pulled him closer. Covering her mouth with his was like an automatic response. Somewhere in the back of his mind a semi-sane thought urged him to go gentle. Ease into the kiss. But he'd been dreaming about kissing this woman and couldn't find his balance now that the time was here.

Instead he lost himself in the pleasure that was all Summer. Lost what was left of his mind in the softness of her lips. To the firmness of her breasts pressed against his chest. To the curve of her hip as his hand roamed up her back. Without thinking, he fisted his hands in her hair and tipped her head back, allowing himself access to feast on her full lips. With a flavor like spun honey.

Plunging his tongue inside her mouth, he gratefully took whatever she offered. He licked and nipped and tangled his tongue with hers in a frenzy of erotic moves. She moaned deeply, a sexy sound, and mimicked his moves.

Her inhibitions spurred him on, as she flipped off his hat and dug her fingers into his hair, holding his head in place. His heart thudded wildly in his chest while he slid his hand up under her shirt and shoved her bra aside. Her skin was hot, all firm satin and pulsating silk. When she arched her back and thrust her breasts forward, he pebbled a nipple between his fingers and listened while her breathing quickened.

Hard as a rock and straining against his jeans, he broke off the kiss and trailed a string of kisses along her jaw and down her neck. He totally lost track of the world around them. Forgot all about her being thrown from the horse. Forgot everything but what he'd wanted to do to her— what he'd dreamed of them doing together. He'd longed for this taste of heaven. Night after night. Fed his fantasies as he was now feeding his senses.

His fingers absently moved to the buttons on her shirt. He had the top three undone when she planted her hands on his chest and pushed. A second went by before he rearranged his brain cells enough to understand.

Dropping his hands, he leaned back. "What's wrong?"

Her face was a grimace of pain. "My ankle. I...I can't stand up anymore."

Dang. Here he'd been seducing the hell out of a woman who had probably broken her ankle. He'd let himself get so carried away he hadn't paid a bit of attention to her possible injuries.

Now wasn't that just the ultimate picture of control?

Chapter 10

Travis was well on his way to regaining self-control as they waited under a stand of trees for the chopper to pick them up. Having the helicopter take them to the clinic in Gideon would shave off a good two hours from the trip instead of going by Jeep. But the silent tension yawning between him and Summer wasn't helping his nerves or his guilt.

Admittedly, he had it bad for the woman. And he hadn't felt this horny since high school. But throwing good sense out the window for Summer when he knew she'd be leaving soon was just plain stupid.

The situation was becoming intolerable. He didn't want to let the days slide by and watch her leave. Why was she so set on leaving soon, anyway? Why couldn't she stay long enough for the two of them to get to know each other—a lot better?

Out of pure desperation for more time with her, he'd

been busy formulating a plan to keep her here. He was only asking for a little extra time, not forever. But if he outwardly pushed her too hard and she stayed, even if it was for his and Jenna's sakes, she'd be miserable, and he'd be back where he'd been with his ex. A huge mistake. Been there, done that.

But really, what would a few more weeks—or months—hurt? She could stay on as housekeeper after Rosie left.

"I still think it would've been easier if we'd ridden double on your horse," Summer gritted out. She tried to hide a wince while she shifted her bottom to a more comfortable position, but he saw the pain reflected in her eyes before she looked away.

"With you barefoot?" He took a deep breath and scowled. "We could have done it that way, yes. But riding double probably would've caused you a hell of a lot more pain than you're already feeling. I'm not okay with that."

"Are you sure the mare will be all right?"

"She's fine. Now that the saddle's off her back, the whole episode is probably forgotten." But Travis wasn't feeling nearly as fine as the mare seemed. The sight of Summer hitting the dirt under the horse's hooves would haunt him for a long, long time.

"How's the ankle?" He'd removed her boot as soon as he'd gotten his head on straight and carried her to the nearest shade. But now he noticed how much the ankle had swelled, and how dark purple bruising was becoming more evident with every passing minute.

"It hurts a little." Grimacing, she tried to move the injured foot. "Mostly, I feel like I need a bath." She couldn't hide the pain from him. He knew she was lying.

He leaned in and slid his arm around her shoulders to give her strength. But the minute he touched her, his own body went weak. His knees started to tremble and his eyes welled. *He'd come close to losing her for good.*

Stunned by his own too-intimate thoughts, he walked them back in his mind and decided it was just the lust sparking between them that was causing him to lose control. And the two of them should do something about that soon. Very soon.

Sucking up some strength of his own, he muttered, "I should've made sure aspirin was in the first-aid kit before we left." He should've done a lot of things differently.

"None of this was your fault, Travis. If anyone was to blame, it was no doubt me. Where did I go wrong, anyway? I thought the mare and I were getting along fine."

"You didn't do anything wrong. Neither did the mare. The saddle wasn't cinched properly."

A glimmer of amusement popped into eyes still squinting against the pain. "An equipment malfunction? Just my luck."

Travis didn't believe for a moment that some fool doing a bad job of saddling a horse had anything to do with luck. One of the hands had either been sloppy or had deliberately left the buckle loose. But he wouldn't mention his suspicions to her.

Just then the chopper appeared on the horizon, and he found a way to change the subject. "Here we go. You and I will be at the clinic in less than twenty minutes."

"I still say I don't need a medical clinic. The ankle is probably just sprained."

"We aren't taking any chances, sugar. An X-ray will let us know for sure."

"What about the horses? You aren't going to leave them here, are you?"

He flicked a glance toward the horses, quietly munching on grass, and shook his head. "The Bar-C foreman,

Barrett, is coming in with the chopper. He'll see that they get back to the barn safe and sound."

Barrett was a rock. Travis thought he should take lessons on safekeeping from Barrett. What good was being the boss if the people he cared about the most weren't safe and sound?

Whoa. What? *People he cared about the most?*

For cripes sake, why was he having such thoughts about Summer? They barely knew each other. One kiss didn't change that. Even one over-the-top, spectacular kiss.

Hmm. He came to the too-eager conclusion that these odd thoughts of protection and intimacy must stem from continued physical frustration and his need. He wanted her worse than he could ever remember wanting a woman. He'd stayed away from sex for far too long. Summer had been the first to tempt him in a good, long while. Still, he didn't think coming on to her too hard or too fast was the right thing to do either.

Dang. He would need some time to consider the ramifications of all this. And he intended to take that time. Just as soon as he finally accomplished the one right thing he should've done from the start—taking care of Summer.

Summer had to chuckle, remembering Travis's overly solicitous behavior. Through the entire ordeal of flying to the clinic and waiting for X-rays, he hadn't left her side. He'd kept at least one hand on her the whole time. The X-ray technician practically had to pry Travis's fingers off her shoulder to get the pictures.

It seemed clear to her that Travis must be blaming himself for the accident. Rather foolish of him. She was an inexperienced rider, for heaven's sake. It had only been an accident.

Now that they were home and she'd been soaking in a

hot bath for a good hour, the aches and pains were nearly gone and her thoughts were free to wander back to their kiss. But when she really thought about their lips touching, and how that had set off fireworks inside, her whole body went weak.

What woman wouldn't go weak at the idea of kissing Travis?

He was special. Kind. Respected. Exciting.

And as sexy as any man she'd ever met.

Darn it. It was too dangerous for her to be so attracted to her boss. But she couldn't help herself.

The last thing she needed right now was to be going gaga over a man. Especially the man she'd been using to reach her goal.

Admittedly, she wasn't much closer to reaching her goal than she had been when she'd arrived. She had discovered that Bobby "Hoss" Packard was in Chance—or nearby. That was something. And she'd seen him, but unfortunately he'd seen her, too. Yet she still had no idea who he was or where to locate him.

For a while she'd had the idea of going to the sheriff for help in finding the guy. But then, Travis hadn't seemed too keen on this sheriff. And she trusted Travis's opinion. He'd lived here all his life.

Summer had faith that something else, some other way of locating the man, was bound to turn up eventually. She just hoped Travis wouldn't mind if she stayed on the ranch long enough to gather more information.

Lounging back in the oversize tub in Travis's master bath, her thoughts immediately went to him. What a man he was. He'd given her a job and a place to stay. He'd rescued her from a situation that could've injured her much worse or even killed her beneath the horse's hooves. He'd even run her a bath.

That had to be the sweetest thing anyone had ever done for her. He was such an enigma. Controlling but kind. Hard to understand.

Back to daydreaming about their kiss, she flipped on the hot-water faucet to warm the bath again. Heat spread through the water, sending bubbles and warmth crawling up the inside of her thighs. The sensation almost made her giggle. And then, it didn't. The feeling was suddenly intense.

Glancing at the back of the bathroom door, halfway open to Travis's bedroom, she thought of him on the other side. He'd said he would take a quick shower and then stand by to see if she needed his help to climb out of the tub. She needed him, all right.

Tentatively testing her ankle, she'd found what she had suspected all along. It was a simple sprain that only hurt when she put weight on that foot. Otherwise, there was hardly any pain at all. She'd appreciated the doctor wrapping it in an elastic bandage and had accepted the set of crutches he'd offered. So far she hadn't even needed to take an aspirin.

The warmer the water grew around her, the more acutely aware she became of the way her own body was betraying her. She'd felt the same kind of prickly sensations when Travis had asked if she needed any help stripping off her torn and dirty clothes. The look in his eyes then had set off a dangerous thrill of anticipation throughout her body. A type of longing to reach for the magic that she was sure would be waiting in his bed.

She'd turned him down then, needing the bath. But she wondered what it would take to put that look back into his eyes.

Nothing like the present to find out.

She pulled the plug on the drain and eased up, standing

on her good foot. Being upright on one leg proved easy enough as she reached for the clean T-shirt she'd been intending to use as pajamas. The shirt just came down to the bottom of her hips. That should stimulate Travis's imagination.

Thinking of it caused her nipples to harden against the material of the shirt. *Whoo, boy.* If she couldn't catch his attention like this, she didn't deserve anyone as wonderful as Travis.

Opening her mouth to call out to him, she found her voice had gotten rusty and the only sound she could make was a pathetic squeak. Clearing her throat, she swallowed hard and fought to lower her tone.

"Travis? Are you out there? I need help."

One second. Two. And the door swung open.

He was clean-shaven and his hair was still wet from the shower. The only clothes he wore were his jeans, and they were slung low on his hips. Her voice left her again.

Somehow, his bare feet turned her on almost as much as the sight of his chest hair.

"You're out of the tub," he said, as his eyes took in the T-shirt and then shot to her chest.

When the direction of his glance slowly rose up her throat and reached her eyes, she met his gaze—and didn't say a word. She could see his mind matching the direction of her thoughts.

It was his turn to clear his throat. But to his credit, he strove to do what he thought was the right thing. "Want me to bring the crutches?"

"In a moment. But first, could you help me with the elastic bandage?" The bandage was still sitting on the bathroom counter and was the first thing she'd spotted to use as an excuse.

"Um, sure." He picked it up and then blinked a couple of times. "You'll need to sit down."

He glanced around the bathroom. "Uh…" Apparently deciding nothing in here would be appropriate, he bent over and picked her up, cradling her in his arms. "Hold on."

Sure thing. In fact, she would be happiest never letting go.

He carried her into the bedroom and gently set her down on the edge of the bed. "You okay there?"

"Mmm."

Kneeling on one knee on the carpet before her, he bent his head to the task of rewrapping the bandage. "Does it hurt very badly?"

"Not at all." But the sight of his muscled shoulders and back, so close and yet so far, was killing her.

Leaning closer, she breathed in the scent of him. He smelled clean, all male, and aroused. *Whew.*

Lifting her hands, she succumbed to temptation and wrapped her fingers lightly around his biceps. He jerked as if he'd been shot and looked up at her.

They were so close she could see the pulse beat at the base of his throat. She was nearly positive she could also see a cloud of testosterone wafting off him and aimed in her direction.

"Sugar?" The darkened look in his eyes shot yet another thrill zinging straight through her veins to heat her from the inside out. "You sure?"

"Yes, Travis, I'm sure."

Her words didn't spur him to movement, so she tried again. "We've got a perfectly good bed right here. And you know we've been heading in this direction for days."

"Weeks…months." He added his own highly exaggerated number to her assessment. "But…"

"Don't. I don't want to think of the reasons why not. Not now. It's been a very long time since I've been in a man's bed. I haven't wanted to. But in your case—I do."

Shaking his head, he laughed in a way that sounded desperate. "I admit we've got…a thing…going on between us. But it's just lust. You're a better person than that."

She noticed he'd said *she* was a better person. But he wasn't? He was weakening. Good.

"I've been through a lot today, Travis. I almost died." Cupping his cheek with her palm, she parted her lips and smiled. "Let's both lose our heads. Just for tonight. What we do will never have to leave this room."

Grimacing, he bit his lip and breathed deeply. But he still didn't move a muscle.

"What about your ankle?" His eyes were shooting sparks of desire that showered her with heat, but that damned hesitation was driving her crazy.

So much for giving him the first move. Summer could scarcely believe she would have to pursue him. Well, she'd wanted a different kind of life, hadn't she? Reaching for the hem of her T-shirt, she lifted it over her head before she could chicken out.

"Dang it," he growled, low and raspy. "That's no fair."

He'd tried to be the good guy. Tried to do the right thing. Now he was going to do the wrong thing, and be as bad as he could be.

And it was going to feel so danged good.

He shucked his jeans in record time, without really remembering how he'd done it. All he could see, in his mind and in front of his eyes, was the image of Summer lifting her shirt. And then the sight of her perfect breasts, full and bare, with rosy nipples just begging to be kissed.

Those bright blue eyes of hers had turned the color of

a Texas storm as they implored him to take her. Or maybe they were saying, *Let me take you.* Whatever. He intended to enjoy every minute.

Pushing her back to lie under him on the bed, he reached out to the woman of his fantasies. He would never have enough of touching her heated skin. And couldn't wait to taste every inch.

He licked a wet line across one nipple and sank into the perfection that was so brazenly offered. With his heart pumping blood through his body at an unprecedented record rate, he took the other nipple into his mouth and suckled. But his hands were everywhere else. Roaming over hot silk, stroking and petting and stirring.

Clenching and unclenching her hands, Summer began to moan and toss her head. He reared his head up just to see her in the throes of passion. She was a picture. Covered by a sheen of perspiration, her eyes had rolled back in her head, and her parted lips looked plumped and wet.

Travis leaned up and nipped at those lips—because he couldn't resist. Returning to her chest, he scraped a kiss along the tender underside of her breasts, and then moved lower to ring her belly button with his tongue. She made a growling sound and went nuts, gathering strength he didn't know she possessed to physically flip him onto his back.

She wanted to lead? Fine by him. He stopped thinking of her as injured, fisted his hands in the sheets and watched her straddle his hips. A groan came from deep in his chest as she ground herself against him, but he never stopped watching. *This* was the picture he wanted to remember forever. Summer, smiling with a look that shouted glory and power as she rubbed herself against his straining erection.

He had to bite the inside of his cheek to keep his hands

still. The need to reach out for her grew nearly impossible to ignore.

"Summer," he moaned through gritted teeth. "You're killing me here."

With laughing eyes, she planted her palms against his shoulders, leaned down and nipped at each of his nipples. Holy mercy. The pleasure zinged along his spine. He didn't know she had a mean streak. Torture had apparently made her list of things to do to him today.

Gasping and drawing in a harsh breath, he buried his hands in her glorious hair. He fought to indulge her, but he was ready to explode.

Then she raised her head and placed openmouthed kisses along his neck and up to his jaw. Constantly moving, she covered his mouth next, with tongue seeking tongue. The sensation of wet fire, hungry, wet fire, threatened to send him over the edge.

He feasted on her mouth, took as good as he gave. Until she broke the kiss, moved up and offered her nipple as a replacement. Oh, yeah. Latching on, he bit and sucked and lathed, lost in the sensation of honey. Flicking his tongue back and forth over the hardened tip, he wanted to drag every bit of pleasure out of it for both of them.

Her panting gasps and heavy breathing told him he must be doing something right. But it wasn't nearly enough. He wanted more, and now.

Running his hands down her curves, he gripped her hips with both hands and lifted her up. His mouth refused to relinquish its prize as he flipped her over on her back. But the needy little sounds she made set him back on his heels to stare down at her.

With her eyes half closed in passion and his sundarkened hands silhouetted against her perfect white skin, she was everything he'd ever wanted. Every secret wish. Every boyhood fantasy.

He intended to own this night. Make it something neither of them would ever forget.

Mindful of her injured ankle, he carefully dragged her to the edge of the bed, dropped back on his knees and parted her thighs. She moaned and grabbed handfuls of bedding the same way he had done before.

Yeah, the sounds she was making as he kissed his way across the inner thigh sent him to ecstasy. He headed straight to his goal: the nest of baby-soft curls at the apex of her legs. Flicking his tongue across the nub at her core, he gorged himself on her taste. Bucking against his mouth, she showed him her approval and demanded more by grabbing his hair and firmly holding him in place.

Ah. Power. Power to take her wherever she needed to go. He licked and sucked and…possessed her.

"Travis." Screaming his name, her voice hit a peak.

As her spasms rolled across his tongue, he regretted not being able to see the expression on her face. But that was only a fleeting thought as the need to please her shot through him like the bullet from a .45. He loved how she went wild with her passion. It was exhilarating and exquisite.

Reluctantly, he left her sweet nectar and lifted his head. She was struggling to breathe as he pulled them both backward onto the bed. He couldn't take his eyes off her angelic face. And decided he'd been wrong before. *This* was the picture he would always remember.

Opening her eyes, she reached out to him with limp arms. "Travis," she murmured sexily. "Come here."

"Not enough?" he asked with a grin.

"Not nearly enough." She touched his chest and the electricity rocketed straight to his gut.

"Hang on." He leaned over the edge of the bed and ripped open the drawer on the bedside table.

Hoping to hell these things didn't have an expiration date, he rummaged around blindly looking for the box of condoms that had been there since before his wife left. He'd never opened the damn box, as he recalled. But those times weren't anything he wanted to think about now. Now was all about unfinished business and the woman who'd been the cause of him losing his mind.

Getting lucky, he located the box without looking and tore it open. Finally, packet in hand, he turned his full attention back to Summer.

Mercy, just look at her. With all that luxurious hair spread out under her head like the wash of a spotlight, she was a sight to behold. He splayed a hand over her creamy-white stomach and sighed.

Looking up at him through half-lidded eyes, she licked her lips and smiled, and he was done. He covered himself quickly and situated himself between her legs.

"I've wanted this since the day I met you," she whispered, digging her fingers into his shoulders. "Hurry, please."

He barked out a half laugh, half sob and loomed over her. "Yes, ma'am."

When he'd lowered himself into position, she hooked her legs around his thighs. He reached between them, testing her readiness and found her still slick and swollen. That was all the sign he'd needed.

As he pressed his erection against her opening, she lifted her hips and met him. "Now, Travis."

Thrusting deep, he got lost in a thrill of sensations. The feeling of being home inside her warm and pulsating body. She was tight yet welcoming in a way he'd never known.

Her moans and pleadings were like throwing gasoline on a fire. He could lose himself forever in the feel of her.

He slid his hands under her bottom and lifted her hips, going deeper yet. A sudden primal urge overtook his resolve to make this the best for her. Every pleasure was magnified in his mind as he pumped in and out, craving release.

He'd thought he was long past noticing anything, but he felt her stiffen underneath him. She keened out his name and clung to his neck as she went over the edge.

Seconds later he followed her on a roller coaster of release, heading straight into oblivion. He experienced the wildest ride of his life.

Chapter 11

Outside in the darkness, the same angry man stood watching as the lights went out upstairs at the big Chance house. The ranch was settling down for the night. But he was wide awake and itching to get started, just now thinking up his new plans for tomorrow.

Man, that was fun today. Especially the look on Travis's face when his slut of a girlfriend, the crazy one, had come limping back to the ranch on crutches. It was worth the chances he'd taken to make sure her saddle would slip.

Too bad she hadn't broken her neck.

But that panicked look from Travis had told him what he needed to know. He was definitely on the right track. That bitch really meant something to the powerful and mighty owner of the Bar-C. From now on, she'd be the target.

Turning to slink out to the moonless range, the man felt slightly dizzy. But he tossed the feeling off as giddiness coming from his success so far. All his problems, every one of them, proved that he had a right to get even.

His life was in shambles. His lover gone. His job hanging by a thread.

Screw Travis Chance and anyone he cared about. So far the pranks were working and annoying the bastard. But the Bar-C hadn't seen anything yet.

"Where's Travis this time?" Summer gingerly walked into the kitchen with barely a twinge of pain and found Rosie finishing up washing the dishes.

It had been several days since the debacle with the horse and she no longer needed the crutches. Today she could return to work full time, according to the doctor.

"Travis flew to Dallas this morning to interview a woman for the full-time housekeeper's job," Rosie told her as she put away the last of the plates. "He'll be back later tonight. How're you doing?"

"Almost well. See?" Concentrating, she walked across the kitchen floor without the limp. "It doesn't hurt at all anymore when I walk on it."

She wished she could say her mind was as well as her ankle. Travis had insisted she stay in bed or on the couch since her fall. That might've been okay if he'd volunteered to stay with her, but he'd needed to work and had left for a two-day business meeting out of town. For the first twenty-four hours, her mind had stayed occupied with thoughts of him and the spectacular night they'd had.

Thinking about it now, she flinched with the memories. *Multiple times.* She'd come for him so many times she had lost count.

Their night had been so intense that she'd started to wonder if she could live through another like it. But she wanted an opportunity to try.

However, the longer Travis stayed away, the more she became convinced that the whole thing had been a mistake. Her gut told her that he'd needed some distance and that was why she'd seen so little of him. Well, he was probably right.

He was her boss. And in a league far out of her reach. She knew that. Still, she'd hoped they could have a few more nights before it was over.

Sighing inwardly, she resigned herself to accepting what was for the best. Any more nights like that one and her guilt about lying to him would no doubt kill her. She could just imagine spitting out the whole truth while in the throes of passion—only to have him kick her off the ranch for good.

So, for the last few days she'd read a little and watched some daytime TV, and her mind had been free to wander elsewhere during the day. A new set of nightmares had kept her from getting much sleep.

Fully expecting nightmares about falling off horses, she'd been surprised when her dreams were of a man named Hoss instead. The man she'd been trying to find had suddenly become the star of her nighttime terrors. The old nightmares she'd had, the ones of *that* night, had been replaced. Now her nights were filled with images of her target turning things around and coming after her. *She'd become his target.*

She'd always figured that because this Hoss guy had run away from the scene and disappeared right before the house burned to the ground, he must've ducked out so he wouldn't get caught by the police like his buddy. That was one of the big reasons why she'd had the nerve to come after him alone. She considered him a coward, not a fighter. But what if he decided to stop running for good and take a stand?

The P.I. she'd hired back home had hinted that he'd found the man in Chance because the guy had grown up near here. She remembered being completely stunned that the P.I. had found him at all when the cops couldn't. But then, in truth, the local cops had given up on him fairly quickly. Instead they'd worked to compile a foolproof case against the other man and mop up their mob investigations with the FBI at the same time.

The more she'd tried to work with her hometown police to identify and capture Hoss, the more they'd become convinced that her nemesis was not the leader of the two. The harder she pushed, the more they became convinced she was losing her mind.

All of that confusion made the second guy seem less important to the police's investigation. Apparently, the first man, the one now sitting in prison for life, had hired his comrade as muscle for the home invasion. It seemed her target hadn't even been a real member of the mob the night they'd broken into her house.

But he *was* the one who'd tied her up and blindfolded her in the basement. She would never forget his face. It had haunted her long enough.

"If you really feel okay, can you do me a favor?" Rosie folded away the dish towels and drew Summer back to the present.

Summer needed to stop rehashing that night and find a way to banish these dreams of the culprit coming after her. The nightmares seemed more crazy than usual. Was it because of the night she'd spent with Travis? It had certainly been a wild and crazy night. One she would never, ever forget. But she had to find some way of getting sleep real soon.

"Sure," she told Rosie. "What can I do for you?"

"My fiancé has asked me to go with him to San Angelo

for a few days so we can locate a house or apartment for rent." Her face turned a shade of blush-pink. "There are only a couple of weeks left till the wedding. Would you be willing to take charge of Jenna while I'm gone? Make sure she goes to school, eats right and gets enough sleep?"

"I'd be happy to take care of Jenna." Happy might have been a small exaggeration, but the little girl was needy and Summer still wanted Rosie as a friend. "Anything you need, just let me know." Summer beamed at the other woman, who seemed so in love. "How'd you two meet, anyway?"

Rosie placed her palm against her heart, and her eyes took on a dreamy look. "We dated in high school, but his parents didn't want us to be together and forced us to break up. He left town a few years later, joined the army and was kicked out, got married and divorced a couple of times. He managed to find him himself some real trouble and spent a year or two in prison. But a while after he was released he came back to Texas. That was a few years ago, and eventually he contacted me."

"And you don't care about his past?"

"He's a good man at heart, Summer. He had a rough childhood and it drove him to do bad things. But he's changed. Both his parents are gone now, and he's trying to make up for the two of us losing so much time."

Summer could see how much in love Rosie was. The warmth of that love spilled out all over and covered everyone nearby. Summer found herself wishing for someone who loved her enough to come for her after so many years and miles. The idea was more than sweet. It was compelling. A sudden streak of jealousy wriggled into her mind before she could banish it.

She had to clear her throat to speak. "Go along. I'll handle everything around here."

"Thanks," Rosie said with a warm smile. "I'll take the old Jeep into town and meet him at Travis's aunt's place. Can you ask Travis if it's okay to leave the Jeep there until I get back?"

"I'm sure Travis won't mind. I'll talk to him when he gets in."

Rosie surprised her and leaned forward for a bear hug. "You've sure become a friend to all of us. I'm real glad your car broke down so we could get to know you."

Summer's jealousy was immediately replaced by a thread of pathetic guilt. Guilt caused by that half lie she'd been telling them. That lie stood between her and the wonderful people she'd been using to gain what she wanted.

After bidding goodbye to Rosie, she sauntered out to the barn, hoping to find a way to repay her debt to everyone by learning more about the ranch. Travis would like that. Plus, she needed to find more in common with Jenna. But guilt continued to weigh heavily on her shoulders, and useless regret refused to leave her in peace.

Exhausted but still on her feet, Summer put a pan of mac-and-cheese in the oven and finished setting the table for herself and Jenna. Thinking of Jenna, she wondered why the child had been so quiet for so long.

When she'd picked her up after school, Jenna had seemed sullen and withdrawn. Summer had tried talking to her, but Jenna would only whine about having too much homework and how she would rather spend her afternoon in the barn. Over a quick snack in the kitchen, Summer had volunteered to help with the homework, but Jenna had refused, saying her daddy wouldn't approve of anyone helping with her lessons.

But that had been well over an hour ago. Jenna was

only seven. They couldn't give a child that age more than an hour's worth of homework, could they?

A wayward thought occurred to her: maybe Jenna had sneaked out of the house to see her horse. Summer didn't want to believe the little girl would resort to sneaking around. Jenna seemed much more outspoken than that. But all things were possible.

Heading up the stairs, Summer crossed her fingers and hoped she would find that Jenna had fallen asleep over her books, instead of having gone out to the barn. She would certainly hate having to reprimand the poor kid for lying. That would be one of the most hypocritical things she could do. It gave her the shakes just to think of it.

Summer wasn't sure she'd been getting through to Jenna up until now. After searching for ways to help her through what was sure to be a difficult period of adjustment now that Rosie was leaving, Summer found herself empathizing with the child.

She also thought she should be doing a better job of becoming a friend Jenna could count on. After all, a mother with no child should be able to relate to a child with no mother.

Peeking into her room, she was dismayed to find the girl's schoolbooks scattered over the bed, but no Jenna in sight. *Darn.* No way could Summer face a confrontation in the barn now. She was too tired tonight.

Then she heard what sounded like murmured voices coming from the walk-in closet. Was someone here with Jenna?

Fortunately, the tone of those voices didn't sound like distress. So if someone was here, Jenna had invited them in. But how could they have arrived without Summer knowing about it? There wasn't any back door to the upstairs, and the only two balconies were off her and Travis's rooms. With no easy way up.

Curious and a little afraid of who or what she would find, Summer tiptoed to the closet and stood behind the door that was ajar. Peeking around the edge of the door into the half darkness of the closet, she let her eyes adjust. She had no trouble spotting Jenna, sitting on the floor all alone.

So what about the voices? Just as the thought occurred to her, she watched as Jenna lifted a rag doll in her arms, cradled it and began crooning to the baby doll with sing-song words. But hadn't Rosie said Jenna didn't like dolls?

Confused, Summer stilled and tried to listen.

"You're okay, baby," Jenna whispered to the doll. "We have a daddy who loves us. And even if everybody else leaves us behind, even if Daddy goes too, I'll be here to take care of you. You won't be alone. I promise."

A single tear slipped down Summer's cheek as her heart went out to the little girl. She knew how terrible it was to feel alone in the world. How could she stand here another minute and let this innocent child's heart keep breaking?

Softly clearing her throat to announce her presence, she waited until Jenna turned around before saying anything. "Jenna? I missed you downstairs."

She'd been half-afraid the girl would be mad at her for eavesdropping, but Jenna just blinked up at her and said nothing. Kneeling beside her, Summer wrapped her arms around her and enclosed her in what she hoped felt like a safe embrace.

"Are you unhappy because Rosie is getting married and leaving?"

Jenna buried her face in Summer's shoulder and shook

her head. "No. Baby Jane is. She's scared. But she's just a crybaby."

"Is this Baby Jane? She looks awfully young to me. How come I didn't know about her?"

Leaning back so she could look up at her, Jenna said, "I didn't tell you. I didn't tell anyone. Baby Jane stays in the closet."

"But, why? She's pretty. Why keep her in the closet?"

"Mama gave me Baby Jane when I was little. I didn't want Daddy to know I still had her. He was real hurt when Mama left us. You…you won't tell him?"

Summer couldn't help herself; she hugged Jenna close to her breast. "No, I won't tell anyone if you don't want me to." She sniffed back the welling tears. "So, you come in here and sing to your doll when you both get scared?"

"Maybe."

"You know, sometimes I get scared, too."

"You do?" Jenna looked thoughtful for a moment. "You could come here and hold Baby Jane if you want."

Summer felt the smile breaking through her tears and opened her heart without thinking. "Thank you. But I'd rather you and me hold on to each other when we're scared. Think that would be okay?"

Another thoughtful moment passed. "That would be okay," Jenna answered quietly.

Summer bit her lip and took a deep breath. "Are you getting hungry? It's almost dinnertime."

Jenna nodded. "Can I go to the barn first?"

"I was hoping we could go out there together after dinner. Your daddy's foreman gave me lessons on taking care of the horses today, and I wanted to show you what I learned. Think you could check on my progress?"

Without answering, Jenna reached up and hugged her neck. Summer choked back the sob that threatened.

Somehow, she and this lonely little girl had crossed a barrier today. And she wasn't too sure she was worthy.

Travis was tired and cranky by the time he got back to the ranch. It was late. On the way home he'd stopped at Stockard's garage and then swung by and checked on his aunt. She was always "doing just fine" whenever he asked. But the older woman lived alone and didn't have any children of her own, so he liked letting her know he'd be there if she needed him.

Tonight Auntie June's attitude was not the problem. She had several friends over at her house playing cards, and she was in good spirits. It was as he left her house that Travis had gotten a call from his foreman, asking for a rare late-night meeting outside the family's barn. That could mean a big problem.

Travis knew danged well his second in command would be up tomorrow long before the sunrise to start his day. Chores and emergencies on a ranch didn't slow down just because a cowboy was tired.

So Travis had agreed to meet with Barrett because whatever the foreman needed at this hour, it would be important.

As he stepped out of his SUV and turned, Travis spotted Barrett waiting for him across the yard. He walked over, wishing he'd had a chance to stop in and check on Summer and Jenna first. Maybe whatever problem Barrett had wouldn't take too long to solve.

"Good evening, Barrett. You're working late tonight."

Barrett Johnson was only a few years older than Travis, but he'd been working for the Bar-C for as long as Travis could remember. Tall and lean, grizzled from years of working the cattle, Barrett made the perfect picture of a

Texas cattleman. Travis wasn't sure how he'd do his job without him.

Barrett shook his hand. "Glad you're back, boss. And it's not so late. A few minutes ago I sent a couple of the hands out to make nightly rounds. I do them myself most nights, but I needed to speak to you tonight."

"Is this going to take a while? Want a cup of coffee?"

Barrett cleared his throat and shook his head. Travis expected a grin out of his old wrangler friend. But the man's expression was stone-cold sober tonight. Uh-oh.

"This won't take long. I just wanted to catch you up on a couple of things."

"Like what?"

"Well, first off, you were right about those saddle cinches you asked me to check the other day. I finally caught a moment to really inspect them. And sure enough, the two right-side cinches had been tampered with. Neatly sliced, right through the leather. Someone wanted to make it look like normal wear. But as you know, we inspect for normal wear every day, so I looked closer."

"And you're sure?"

"Oh, yeah. Someone took the time to make dozens of almost invisible cuts in the leather, so that any sudden forceful movement by the rider would make the leather slip and slide on the horse's back. Sneaky. Good thing you'd asked for the most docile mare we own. Any other horse would've killed the rider to get that saddle off."

Yeah, that's what Travis had been afraid of. "Any ideas concerning who would do such a thing?"

"I questioned the two hands I'd asked to saddle the horses that day, but they didn't notice any wear as they did the job. They've both been with us for years, boss. It wasn't them."

"Okay. Well, the culprit will turn up sooner or later." He turned to head for the warmth of the kitchen.

"Uh, that's not all of it," Barrett called after him.

Travis turned back and felt a chill having nothing to do with the night air rolling down his spine. "What else?"

"We've suddenly had a series of small *accidents* around the ranch. The electric lights on a stock pond were cross wired and nearly electrocuted one of our prize Santa Gertrudis bulls. Then your brother Sam's head horse wrangler, riding his best stallion, tangled himself up in a roll of barbed wire that shouldn't have been left out on the range."

"Was he hurt badly?" Barbed wire was dangerous stuff. Deadly when used wrong and easy to miss on an open range.

"Lucky. Both rider and horse. Turned out the wrangler needed over a hundred stitches, but he's back to work now. His horse, on the other hand, only needed a few stitches and had simple bruises down his foreleg from the fall. Most wranglers would rather save their horse than themselves."

Travis definitely did not like the idea of these *little* accidents happening all at once. "Get the word out. Everyone needs to be super-careful for a while. You and I will start an investigation into who might've had the opportunity or would've wished the Bar-C harm."

"Listen, boss, I think…"

At that moment the sound of one of the hands yelling came from somewhere around the other side of the barn and caught their attention. The two of them headed off at a run to find out what was wrong and found the cowboy frantically waving at them.

"The newest foal!" the hand said on a gasp. "The little girl's pride and joy. I think she's dying!"

Barrett took him by the arm and squeezed hard enough to force the man to pay attention and calm down. "What exactly happened and where is the filly now?"

"Someone left the feed-storage room open. The door we're always supposed to lock up for the night. It's wide open and the foal's inside, rolling on the floor!"

Travis didn't wait to hear the rest. A horse that overeats could easily give itself colic, and colic was well known as a potential killer of horses. Especially for one that was barely weaned.

"Get the vet out here now," Travis yelled over his shoulder as he headed for the feed room.

As he ran, his thoughts weren't on the colicky foal, but on Jenna. His little girl had been acting subdued lately. He'd recognized the signs. She was worried about Rosie's leaving. But he hadn't known what to do to help.

Mercy. How much worse would it be if her little horse died, too?

Chapter 12

Summer sat straight up in bed, shoving aside the cobwebs still clogging her brain from another terrifying nightmare. What a dream. Her quarry, Hoss, had been chasing her. And as he was about to catch up, she fell into a deep hole and woke up.

Tremors rocked her body and her stomach churned with the remnants of nighttime terrors. A quick glance at the clock on the bedside table told her it was past 1:00 a.m. Throwing back the covers, she scrambled to the side of the bed, needing desperately to put her feet on solid ground.

Sitting at the edge, feet firmly planted on the floorboards, she buried her head in her hands and took long, slow breaths in and out. Was she dissolving back into the madness that had kept her captive for so long after the murders? But why? She felt sure she'd been cured. Even though the doctors had told her that it might take many more years.

She sorted through all the things she'd learned over the last few years of talking to professionals that might help now. Her last psychologist had said extreme stress could send her right back into therapy. But she didn't feel stressed. Not at all. It felt as if someone was chasing her. And that didn't make any sense.

Calm down and think it through.

Could these reeling emotions be due to Jenna, and the idea of a different child holding a spot in her heart where her own daughter's memory belonged? That idea didn't sit quite right either.

Her grief for her lost child continued to this day, fierce and biting. And it probably always would. But she'd finally come to the realization that grief could be manageable, and believed she'd dealt rather successfully with the worst of the pain—except for the lingering guilt. Obviously, however, she hadn't solved all her problems. Something new must be causing the nightmares.

Maybe it had to do with her growing attraction to Travis. Since their night of making love, it had become more and more frustrating to have to keep telling herself she would be leaving the ranch someday soon. Frustration? Yes, on several fronts. At not seeing Travis for more than a few minutes at a time since their one night. And at not being able to tell him the truth about why she'd originally come to the ranch. And…at not yet finding her man.

Hadn't she heard somewhere that frustration could wreak havoc with the nervous system if it became a constant state? And she definitely remembered one of her earliest psychologists cautioning her to keep her body healthy. He'd said staying physically fit would help ease the terrible frustration she'd felt at not being able to save her child. Exercise was the key.

Only one kind of exercise interested her lately.

Drawing in a deep breath and fighting the nausea from leftover anxiety, Summer tried to stand on shaky legs. She needed to get out of this room and its dark shadows. Finally, not feeling too steady but at least upright, without turning on the light, she grabbed her old robe and tore out into the hall.

She considered having a warm glass of milk; another way of lessening nighttime stress she'd learned from one of her doctors. It might be worth a try. And besides, she was always happiest while in the kitchen.

Tiptoeing down the staircase so as not to wake Travis and Jenna, she made her way to the back of the house. But as she approached the kitchen, she saw light streaming from under the door. Voices came from the other side.

Someone else was up at this hour? Was something wrong? The hair on the back of her neck stood straight up as she came nearer the kitchen door.

She felt sure that if it was something very bad, Travis would've awoken her. Not willing to barge into the middle of trouble without an abundance of caution, she put her ear close to the door and listened.

One of the voices was Travis's; she easily recognized it. And unless she missed her best guess, the other voice belonged to Barrett, the ranch foreman she'd spent the day with learning about the horses. They were keeping their tones low but seemed to be having a disagreement.

"I don't know what you two have going on," Barrett was saying, "but the whole town knows she's...well, if not downright crazy, at least eccentric."

"What do you mean by the *whole town?* If you're talking about Old Lady Wheeler, she's the crazy one." Travis's tone made it sound as if he was on the verge of losing his temper.

"*Everyone's* talking about the weird woman who drove

into Chance all alone in a beat-up heap of a car—without a plan and without any family nearby. That's nuts and you know it. Even the sheriff has been out here a couple of times asking about her. Who else would do something as nutty as that, except a crazy person or maybe someone on the run?"

They were talking about *her.* Summer's pulse kicked up and she had trouble hearing their conversation over the pounding of her heart.

"Summer is not crazy." It sounded as though Travis was gritting his teeth to form the words. "Or weird. Or eccentric. She's had a tough past. But quite a few of the residents in Chance have had just as bad. Some far worse."

Travis's tone dropped to a near whisper. "And as far as the sheriff is concerned, you can tell him the next time you see him that she doesn't drink or do drugs. She's never been in jail. The law's not looking for her, and she doesn't have an abusive ex chasing her. Take my word for it—she would never harm a living soul. I trust her completely."

Why were they having this conversation about her at one o'clock in the morning? Summer didn't understand any of it. Cowering outside the door, she tried to hear more without letting them know she was listening.

"But she *did* do a lot of harm, boss. It had to be her. She and Jenna were the last ones out of the barn tonight. And Jenna knows better than to leave the feed-room door open. In fact, I'm positive I also told Summer about keeping that door closed when I was showing her around this afternoon. But she seemed a little out of it at the time. You know—*whoo-whoo?*"

Left the feed-room door open? Had she? No. She could swear she remembered closing that door. But what had happened to cause all the fuss? Why did it matter? She held her breath and waited to hear what the consequences had been of leaving the door open.

"It wasn't Summer." Now Travis's tone made it sound that at least *he* was convinced, even if she wasn't. "Put that theory out of your head and look for some other reason why the door was found open. I've got my own problems at the moment. The vet said the foal is going to pull through, so at least I don't have to tell Jenna her horse is gone. But I'm probably going to have to tell her it didn't look too good there for a while, and she'll have to stay away from the filly for a couple of weeks until it's completely well."

Jenna's horse? Oh. My. God. Summer felt light-headed, and her knees buckled under her. She slumped hard against the swinging door.

Travis turned to the noise and found Summer collapsing through the doorway to the kitchen floor. "Summer!"

Rushing to her side, he pulled her up off the floor and into his arms. Damn. How much had she heard?

He carried her over to one of the kitchen chairs and slipped her onto the seat. "Hang on. Let me get you a glass of water." He made sure she was propped against the table and wouldn't fall out of the chair.

Turning, he spied Barrett, looking rather helpless while fidgeting on one foot by the back door. "Go see if the vet needs anything else," Travis told him as he ran to the fridge. "Then try to grab an hour or two of sleep. The night's almost gone. We'll start another investigation tomorrow."

"Okay, boss." Barrett's hesitant expression clearly said he was embarrassed that Summer might have heard him calling her crazy.

Travis could not afford to have the best foreman in the

entire state feeling uncomfortable around anyone in the household. It would make the man's job untenable, and Travis had no intention of trying to replace the foreman he'd counted on for nearly eight years over simply a few unthinking words said in the heat of the moment. He also had no intention of letting Summer leave the household. His plan was to keep her on the ranch for as long as he possibly could. Everyone had to get along.

"Stop by tomorrow morning," he told Barrett. "All of us will talk this through. Maybe we can come up with a solution for finding who left the door open."

Barrett sent him an appreciative glance and nodded his head. "I've already stationed a couple of hands in the barn. They're sitting with the vet in case he needs anything else. I'll see you in the morning." Lifting his chin and settling his hat more firmly on his head, Barrett turned and walked out the door.

Travis would work on that little problem more tomorrow. Tonight would be devoted to easing the guilt and pain he knew Summer would be feeling.

Quickly filling a glass with water he went to her side and knelt on the floor beside her. "Here you go." He lifted the glass to her lips as she raised her head.

"No, no, no," she sobbed. "How could I do something so stupid? The whole town must be right. I must be going crazy."

"You're not crazy. Take a little sip, please, so we can talk about this."

He'd been hesitant to tell her of his suspicions that someone was playing nasty tricks on the Bar-C. He'd told himself that the reasons for his silence stemmed from trying his best to shield her from anything dirty and potentially dangerous. But the truth was, he also feared that, if she knew, she might want to leave any potential danger—and him—far behind.

He realized now that in a certain way he'd been trying to control her. And after he'd promised himself he would never do that to anyone again. Especially not to her.

It was past time to come clean and hope she would understand. And *stay,* despite his failings.

She held the glass with trembling hands, but managed to swallow half the water before setting it down. "You don't understand, Travis. I *have* been crazy in the past. I spent two years in intensive therapy, just so I could manage to live on my own again. It's entirely possible I need to go back on the meds. I don't remember leaving that door open, but I *could have.*"

She looked totally miserable, full of self-doubt and blaming herself. He would give up a lot to be able to hold her in his arms and show her that he was convinced she hadn't been at fault. But now didn't seem like the right time for too much intimacy. Not yet. He slipped into another chair and pulled it in as close to hers as possible.

Sliding an arm around her shoulders, he whispered in her ear, "You did *not* leave the door open. Get that thought out of your head. I'm sorry for not telling you before, but I didn't want to worry you. Tonight is only one of a series of supposed accidents around the Bar-C."

"Wh…what do you mean?"

Past time he accepted that she was a capable woman and let her make her own decisions. "Someone has been playing a series of so-called pranks, nasty ones, around the ranch. I thought whoever it was would give up, or we'd find him. But it hasn't stopped, and we aren't any closer to finding the jerk who's been committing these acts of sabotage."

"Nearly killing Jenna's foal doesn't seem much like

a prank." Her eyes were clearing and her breathing was stronger.

"No," he admitted. "And neither was cutting the cinch on your saddle. But someone did that, too."

She gasped and narrowed her eyes on him. "You didn't tell me that my fall wasn't an accident? That's no prank. I could've been killed. It's something I needed to know. Why didn't you say anything?"

"I thought I could keep you safe. I've had Barrett double-checking anything that could harm you before you even think to use it. But now you need to understand the possible danger."

Her mouth turned down in a straight, disapproving line. But at least she seemed to be regaining her balance. Still, he wasn't too crazy about the way she was looking at him.

It took another few seconds for her to say anything. "You can't keep me blindfolded to a situation and locked away in a fantasyland, Travis. I'm not one of the hands you need to control for the good of the ranch. I have to participate in my own life. It's the only way for me to remain sane. Please don't smother me."

"I... Sorry. But I swear I didn't know this particular situation would keep involving you. I'm positive I'm the main target of this guy's criminal acts and you're just suffering by proximity."

She reached up and cupped his cheek with her palm. "Don't be too sure of anything. And even if it's true that someone is out to hurt you, don't you think I'd want to know when you're under a threat? I'm not entirely self-ish. Maybe I could've been on the lookout for someone who's really dangerous."

"Sorry," he mumbled again. He'd had enough talking for now. "We'll find the guy eventually. But can we talk about this tomorrow? You need your sleep. We've only got a few hours till Jenna should be getting up for school."

Summer stared at him in stony silence, and he wondered if she thought he was trying to control the situation again. "Okay. I'm the one that needs sleep. Is that better?"

Chuckling, though the look on her face said she was still miserable, she patted his arm. "We both need it. I'm just not sure I'll be able to rest after all that's happened."

Ideas to help her forget and relax immediately came to mind. In fact, dozens of sensual, enthusiastic ways of helping her forget filled his imagination. But he discarded them all as too intense for her current misery and sucked up a little fortitude. She was exhausted—he knew by the dark circles under her eyes. And he did understand that there were ways to help her relax without sex. Though every one of them would quietly drive him to distraction. But tonight he owed her the peace and quiet. And he vowed to find a way, if not tonight, then for sure tomorrow, to prove to her that she was not crazy.

"Let's head on upstairs. Maybe I'll give you a back rub. That should relax you."

She pushed back from the table while watching him carefully. "I didn't know you gave back rubs. Why didn't you tell me that before?"

"Only very special people get my back rubs." He started to reach out to steady her, only to catch himself and back up a step.

She was too vulnerable. Too sexy in her ratty bathrobe. Any touching might prove his ultimate undoing.

As they walked through the dimly lit hall toward the stairs, her expression changed from tired but determined to exhausted and beat down. He had to get her mind off both the town gossip and the subversion on the ranch.

"I've missed you the past couple of days. Yesterday in

Dallas was the hardest without you. The interview went badly. I sure wished you'd been there to help me."

She turned to him as they came to the bottom of the staircase. "Me? What could I have done to help?"

Her eyes were like two purple bruises looking out at him. It hurt deep down to see her like this.

He lifted a hand to take hold of her elbow and help her climb the stairs. But then he realized that one touch might send him over an edge to a point where he might never recover.

"You're smart," he said as he propped his thumbs in his jeans pockets to keep his hands still. "You would've seen right away that the applicant was unsuited for ranch life. I wasted the whole afternoon with her before she finally asked how far it was from the ranch to the nearest shopping mall."

"How far is it? What'd you tell her?"

He had to smile at the memory of the woman's facial expression. "Her eyes grew wide as dinner plates when I told her it was at least a hundred fifty miles to the nearest mall. That did it for her. She couldn't leave the employment office fast enough."

Summer reared her head back. "Really? Who would've thought?"

Dang, why'd he have to go and tell her that story? He didn't want her thinking about how isolated she was here on the ranch. "If we need to shop for anything we can't get at the Feed and Seed store, it's a forty-five-minute flight by either the Cessna or the helicopter in to San Antonio. Makes a nice day trip."

She nodded, grabbed hold of the banister and continued pulling herself along up the stairs. "That wouldn't be so bad. But I guess your applicant didn't agree."

He hadn't told the woman any such thing. He hadn't

wanted her to feel comfortable coming to the ranch. He flat-out didn't want to hire a stranger. In fact, he didn't want to hire anyone. Not when he was praying for a way to make Summer want to stay.

"Nope. It was a wasted trip, I'm afraid."

Without his assistance, the trip up the stairs seemed to be taking Summer forever. Just when he was feeling guilty about not helping, they reached the top. Summer put a finger to her mouth and nodded toward the door to Jenna's room.

"Let me check on her," she whispered.

He should've thought of that. But right at the moment, Jenna was the last thing on his mind. He stood in the hall a few feet away, while Summer peeked in on his sleeping daughter.

In seconds, Summer quietly closed the door again. "She looks fine. Sleeping soundly. I didn't want to wake her by touching her, but I'm sure she's okay."

He nodded and turned toward the guest room where Summer had been staying. "Good. Now it's your turn. You look exhausted."

"What are you going to tell her about the filly?" Summer hung her head and followed him down the hall.

When he reached Summer's closed door, he realized her lonely room was the last place he wanted to leave her now. But he couldn't think of a good way out without feeling like a sex-starved brute.

He stood back and let her move around him as he answered, "I'll tell her the foal is sick and the vet wants the little filly to be immobilized for a few days. I don't want Jenna anywhere near that barn until her horse is well. Thinking someone might've deliberately hurt her filly could be too scary for a seven-year-old."

Standing with one hand on the doorknob, Summer

looked up into his eyes. "What will you say about the feed-room door?"

Mercy, just look at her. The woman's eyes were so full of anguish, it almost took his breath away. He had to turn his back or he would've gathered her up in his arms for sure.

Scrubbing his hands across his eyes, he answered the best he could without looking at her. "Not that you had anything to do with it, that's for sure. I'll tell her it was an accident. I don't want her worrying about something as awful as sabotage."

With a deep breath, he took a step down the hall and muttered over his shoulder, "Go to bed, Summer. Tomorrow will be soon enough to figure out what to do about Jenna."

He took another step before he realized she'd come up behind him. "You're a good father. Jenna is lucky to have you."

She slipped her arms around his waist and pressed her cheek against his back. "I'm lucky to have you, too. You're our hero, Travis. I'm sorry I said you were too controlling. Both Jenna and I understand you do what you do because you care."

"I've changed since you came," he said as he twisted around in her arms and held her close to his heart. "I question my actions all the time now. I'm trying to let go, but it's danged hard."

Tipping her head back, she looked up at him. "You are a good person. Keep that in mind." Then she slid her arms around his neck and kissed him with so much tenderness, it nearly rocked him out of his boots.

When she pulled back to take a breath, her eyes were glittering and so full of passion he was a goner. No way was he going to watch her walk away now. It would kill him.

Without another word, he lifted her off her feet. Cradling her in his arms, his eyes locked on hers, he turned and carried her off to his bed.

Chapter 13

Travis laid Summer on the bed, turned on the lamp and closed the door. His hands were still shaking. But as he slowly undressed her, letting his fingers linger over every inch of silky skin, he found strength.

He gave his greedy eyes the time to caress her, while he whispered soothing words and let her know what a joy she'd been since she'd come into his life. When they were both naked, he knelt next to her, then moved between her open thighs.

So sweet. Her mouth was tender, hot and welcoming.

Summer slipped her hands up his chest and touched his face, telling him how she felt with her kiss. He responded by filling his hands with her luscious softness, so taken with feeling he could barely breathe.

What a gift for the senses she was. No adrenaline rush this time, he thought inanely. Only pure, raw pleasure in enjoying each other.

As he slid inside her welcoming warmth and made love to her with a tenderness that surprised him, he felt overcome by something so complex he couldn't find words to describe it. Suddenly this wasn't about sex. It was about reverence, and about finding the one right person who could make him feel whole. And good. And right.

He heard her take a breath and looked over to find her crying. But when he reared his head back, she smiled at him through the tears. The look in her eyes said she understood: him, his unspoken emotions, everything. With that one look they were no longer two lost souls, but rather a couple who'd found communion.

And he hadn't even known he'd been looking for someone like that. But he got it. He got the connection. There was nothing left of him and her. From here forward they were a *we*.

As he made love to her with a new intimacy, the heat and intensity followed. And when they were spent and entwined in each other's arms, he realized he'd just been through the most profound emotional experience of his whole life.

He saw things clearly now. The difference between what he felt now for her and anything he'd ever felt before in his life was true love. Oh, he still didn't like the idea of her leaving in the future. He wanted her with him always. But now that he understood what love was really all about, he could see that *her* needs were the most important thing. Not his. If she needed to go—anywhere—anytime, he would let her go. Even if it killed him.

He was in love. Passionately. Irrevocably.

The first rays of sunlight were peeking through Travis's windows when Summer stepped out of the shower with a huge smile on her face and nothing on but a towel.

They'd spent the whole night in his bed—until a half hour ago, when she'd decided she needed a shower. Of course, Travis wouldn't let that happen without joining in the fun.

But now, towel drying her hair as she stood in front of the mirror atop the dresser, she blushed when she thought of all the things they'd done. Travis was everything she'd ever wanted. More than she'd thought she could have. No one had ever treated her with such tenderness or made her feel as special as he did.

But her guilt at lying and using him refused to stay buried. It crept back into her mind and forced her to turn away from her image in the mirror. She stared out the balcony window and thought of him. He was a man's man and too prone to having his own way. But last night, he'd been a tender, solicitous lover. He'd given her everything he had, his body and his heart.

When what she'd been feeling for days now finally clicked in, she straightened her spine and tried to blink back the truth. She was in love with Travis. Totally. For good and for always.

But she couldn't be. That was impossible. After what they'd done together, been together, felt together, what on earth would he do when she told him the truth?

Frantic with worry, she froze on the spot, not knowing which way to turn. This wasn't supposed to happen. Despite her marriage, she'd never really been in love before. But now she faced the ugly truth. She and her husband had only been using each other to get what they needed. He'd needed a respectable wife. And she'd wanted a child to love.

But with Travis it was so much different. How could she have suspected love with him would be this kind of all-consuming, all-powerful condition?

Suddenly, she would do anything—*anything*—not to

see him hurt. But she'd boxed herself into a desperate corner. Nothing she did from here on out would keep him from being hurt. If she left him behind without telling him the truth, he would be hurt. If she told him the truth, he would be hurt knowing she'd lied.

Holding her head in her hands, she closed her eyes and wished the floor would open up and swallow her whole. How could she go on like this?

"Daddy?" Jenna's high-pitched voice came through the closed bedroom door. "Are you awake? It's Saturday. Hurry up downstairs. I need Summer to fix my breakfast so I can go out to the barn."

Jenna! Summer grabbed her robe from the floor. She was putting her arms through the sleeves when Travis came out of the bathroom, wiping remnants of shaving cream off his neck. He was wearing his jeans, boots and nothing else, and looked so sexy that she almost forgot about his daughter at the door.

Almost. "It's Jenna," she told him in a stage whisper.

"I heard." He grinned at her but turned to yell through the door without opening it. "Get dressed, baby. Summer and I will be down in a minute."

"Okeydokey!"

Travis reached for a T-shirt and pulled it over his head. "I think we'd better get down there." He strode the few feet between them and kissed her on the top of the head. "I don't want to take a chance of Jenna scooting outside to see her foal before I can warn her off."

"But…I'm not dressed."

Travis threw his arm around her waist and tugged her close. "You look beautiful. Just come down long enough to fix her breakfast. I intend to rush her over to her Aunt June's as soon as she's eaten, and you can take your time getting dressed then."

"Well, I suppose it'll…"

He bent his head and gave her a kiss that hummed along her skin as the blood boiled in her veins. "I'd much rather go back to bed, too," he mumbled as he backed up and gazed into her eyes. "Or better yet, take that shower all over again. But both of those things will have to wait until tonight. Good enough for you?"

"I… Tonight will have to be okay." It took everything she had to smile at him.

"That's my gal." He turned to walk toward the bedroom door.

"Travis."

Turning back, he grinned in that special way again and almost caused her to forget what she'd wanted to say. "We need to talk. Tonight after everything has calmed down."

"Sure, sugar. I've got a few things to say then, too." He gave her a meaningful look that nearly took her to her knees, then he opened the door. "But right now we need to hustle. Come on."

Against her better judgment, she wrapped the robe around her, tightened the belt at her waist and followed him out the door.

So many things were chasing through Travis's mind as he bounded down the stairs, he almost tripped over his own boots. He'd been planning on telling Summer how much he loved her, but he needed to ensure her and Jenna's safety first.

Tonight, things would be settled and he would tell her, he promised himself. And the image of how he would tell her, and where, sent a warm smile through his veins.

But then the old niggle of worry bored into his brain. He began to wonder if telling her he loved her would be enough to keep her on the ranch. Just talking about love hadn't been enough to keep his ex-wife here.

Thinking back to last night and the punch-in-the-gut sex he and Summer had shared, he knew that had never happened with his ex. It had never happened to him in his entire lifetime.

Summer must love him in the same way. He couldn't be wrong about something so important. That had to be what she'd wanted to talk about.

His chest swelled when he thought about her feeling the same things he did. Dang, but the woman was hot. How had he gotten so lucky?

Still, the problem of isolation on the ranch might yet stand between them. He needed more time with her. With enough time, he could show her all the things to love about the Bar-C and this part of Texas. Already she'd seemed to take to the horses. There were many other things to love around here, too. Including him. All he needed to turn her to his view was a little more time.

A few days ago he'd been plotting out a couple of ways to gain more time. But that was before. Before she had become his life's goal. So, during the day today, he would give a lot more consideration to the best way to make her *want* to stay.

He hit the kitchen door and looked around for Jenna. She wasn't anywhere in sight. Was she still upstairs getting dressed? Didn't feel right.

Then he heard a noise at the back door and knew where she was. Speeding up, he made it to the mudroom just as Jenna put her hand on the doorknob of the outside door.

"Stop!" He was out of breath, but not from running. "I thought I told you to wait for Summer to make breakfast."

His child was already wearing her denim barn jacket and turned to look at him over her shoulder. "No, Daddy.

I said I wanted breakfast, but I changed my mind. I wanna see baby Mumps." Rather than wait for an additional comment she might not like, Jenna opened the door.

"Halt, young lady. Not another step. We need to talk, and you need breakfast."

"But, Daddy…" She turned to him with the precocious kind of pout that usually worked to soften him up.

Not today. "Shut the door. I'll help you out of your coat."

"Aw, shoot. Not fair," she complained, but did as he'd said anyway.

She raised her arms one at a time so he could shake her out of the jacket, which he noted was getting to be too small. It pained him to think about how fast she was growing. But it hurt a lot worse when he thought of telling her about the filly.

Bending down on one knee so he could look her in the eye, he began, "I'm afraid you won't be able to go to the barn today—maybe not at all this week. It's…"

"What? But, Daddy, I'll be good." Tears swelled in his little girl's eyes, grown wide with hurt.

He drew her to him. "It's got nothing to do with you, sweetheart. You're always my best girl. But something bad happened last night. Something that means you'll have to stay away from Mumps this week."

"Oh, no. Is Mumps hurt? She's not…not…dead, is she?"

Children on ranches had to grow up fast and learned about death far too soon. Such as when the pet chickens had been killed by a coyote. Or when the neighbor's 4-H lambs were sold at auction for someone's table. Jenna had already lost an animal or two and knew what *dead* meant.

Travis was real glad this wasn't one of those times. "Mumps is alive. But she's hurting pretty bad. The vet wants to keep her quiet for a few days. Like you had to stay in bed with pneumonia when you were little, remember? So we're going to give her the space to heal."

"What happened to her?" Her sweet blue eyes were as wide as a Texas sky.

This was going to be touchy. "Well, it seems the feed door was accidentally left open last night. Mumps apparently got hungry, wandered inside the feed room and ate until she made herself sick."

Jenna's eyes filled with tears again, and this time her bottom lip quivered. He waited for another question. One that would be harder to answer. But it didn't come.

She shifted on one foot and looked at him hesitantly. He opened his arms wide, expecting her to need a hug. But instead of running into his embrace as she normally would, she turned away and dashed into the kitchen.

"Jenna?" Bolting upright, he quickly followed.

The sight that greeted him as he entered the kitchen's warmth made his heart do somersaults. There, by the sink, was his baby girl, crying her eyes out with her arms around Summer's waist and her face buried against Summer's belly.

He wasn't sure how to feel about that. In a way, it hurt to think he wasn't the one she would run to anymore. But in another way, he was happy that Jenna had found a woman she considered safe—like a mother figure.

His own eyes welled as he listened to her cry. But he balled his fists and stood there waiting.

"And it was an accident," Jenna wailed. "The door was open. But Daddy says she'll…she'll be okay."

Summer stood still, quietly petting Jenna's hair. "Yes, that's what the vet said. We just have to wait."

"I don't want to wait. I want to see Mumps now."

"Jenna…" Summer looked up at him over his daughter's bowed head, her eyes saying she was at a loss for words.

Travis figured that was his cue. "Okay, ladies," he said in the firmest tone he could manage, while walking toward them. "Here's the plan. We're going to have something to eat, and then I'm taking Jenna into town to stay with her Aunt June for a few days."

Jenna whirled at the sound of his voice. "But…" She stopped whining when she looked up into his eyes and saw his determination. "Yes, Daddy. But I'm not going to like it."

"Sure you are. You love going to Auntie June's. She has a whole yard full of toys to play with, and there are a couple of little kids in the neighborhood who go to your school. Plus, I'll bet Rosie will stop by and ask you to practice your part in her wedding."

Jenna brightened. "Do you think so? Really?"

"I'm sure she will. Why don't you run upstairs now and pack your duffel, while Summer finishes making the breakfast?"

"Okeydokey." Jenna turned and disappeared, going a hundred miles an hour toward the stairs.

Summer ran a dish towel under her eyes and said, "That was tough. How do you handle your emotions when your child is hurting?"

He shrugged and took her in his arms. "Not a clue. I've been having a lot of trouble with emotions myself lately. No choice but to do what comes naturally."

"I guess." She flipped her hair off her forehead and sighed.

At least she didn't say she wouldn't be here long enough to find out. A step in the right direction. "You'll get the hang of it," Travis said. "All you need is to love your child. Once you've got that handled, the rest comes easy enough."

"Jenna didn't ask about the accident."

"No, she didn't." And Travis couldn't say how glad that made him. "She might yet. It's possible she'll hear rumors in town from the other kids."

"Oh?" Summer frowned and turned around to face the stove.

"Don't worry. I intend to find the real bad guy before then, sugar. I've had an idea. I'm going to call my brother Gage, the P.I. You met him once, remember?"

She nodded but kept her back turned.

"Gage is a genius at security. He wired my brother's house when my sister-in-law had a stalker. And he's the best at uncovering mysteries, just like Sherlock Holmes. He'll know how to pin down this jerk."

Travis went to the ranch's intercom on the kitchen wall and dialed the foreman's line. "I'll take Barrett with me to town while I drop Jenna off. Afterward, we'll stop by Gage's office. Between me, Barrett and Gage, we'll either be able to figure out who the guy is, or we'll lay a trap and catch us a saboteur."

He made arrangements with Barrett to go to town, then thought of something else. Turning to Summer, he said, "I'm a little concerned about you staying on the ranch without me. It could be dangerous."

"You said you wouldn't try to smother me, Travis. I'm an adult. I'll be fine. You'll still have hands working here, won't you?" She kept her back to him as she took the egg sandwiches she'd made and wrapped them in tin foil.

Heaving a heavy sigh, he gave up. "All right. But promise me you'll stay in the house and away from the barns this morning until I return. And if you need anything—anything at all—use the intercom to call the ranch office. I'll leave the men instructions to come running."

"I said, I'll be fine. Please don't worry about me."

She was asking the impossible, but he kept his mouth shut. He was about to explain his concern to her with another kiss when Jenna rushed back into the kitchen.

"I'm all set. Let's go."

Summer handed her a bag with two sandwiches. "For the road."

"Will I see you later?" Jenna asked.

"Sure you will. I'll be coming into town this week to run errands. I'll stop by your aunt's to say hello."

Jenna grinned, stood on tiptoes and dragged Summer's head down for a kiss on the cheek. "Make sure the vet takes good care of Mumps. Okay?"

"I will. Don't worry."

Jenna grabbed her coat and skipped out the door. He needed to be right behind his daughter.

Twisting around, he gave Summer a quick kiss—much too quick for his liking—and took a step to follow his daughter.

"Don't forget about our date tonight," he said before reaching for the door handle.

"What date?"

"To talk. You haven't forgotten?"

"I haven't forgotten."

"Good." The idea of seeing her again made feel him all warm and mushy inside.

Oh, he wanted her. The lust nipping at his gut was a constant state. But just being around her made him happy—more, it made him feel like a teenager again. Now, how about that?

* * *

Summer finished cleaning the kitchen and trudged up the stairs to finally get dressed. It promised to be a long day without Jenna or Travis around the house.

The endorphins left over from last night had quit bouncing around inside her at about the same time Jenna had come tearing into the kitchen needing a hug and comfort. Then Summer's more lustful hormones had quickly been replaced with a heavy dose of the mothering instinct.

And now that Jenna and Travis had gone, her guilt had come back stronger than ever. She didn't believe anymore that she'd been the cause of the filly's sickness. Travis had convinced her it wasn't her fault. But still, she was here under false pretenses, and it was killing her. While they were gone today, she'd better think over what she wanted to do from here on out.

Everything would be so much simpler if she could only find her man and turn him in. Then she could really think about what she wanted to do with the rest of her life.

She'd been so impressed with the way Travis had handled Jenna this morning. He was basically deep down a good man who loved his child, his ranch and his life. It made her wonder why some smart woman had not already snapped him up since his divorce.

Lost in her thoughts of Travis, and holding back a cascade of love for him so strong it threatened to swamp her, she opened her bedroom door. What she saw next erased everything else but the horror before her eyes.

Her room had been destroyed. Clothes and bedspread lay strewn across the floor. Drawers were left open and askew. Pillows had been shredded to pieces and spread into every corner. A lovely artwork had been removed from the wall and destroyed. Photos of Jenna as a baby were slashed and the frames smashed.

Her first thought was that maybe she'd done this and not remembered. Certainly she'd been crazy enough lately.

But in the next instant, she looked at the mirror over the dresser and saw the words written in what looked like lipstick:

Crazy witch! Die!

That snapped her out of it. She recovered her senses and realized someone else had to have done this. She wasn't crazy, she was better. And in love. She could never have done anything like this.

So who had done it? And where were they now?

Belatedly, she ran to the balcony window and checked the door. It wasn't locked. But no one was out there lurking, either. She locked the balcony door with trembling fingers and spun to the closet.

Had she just locked herself in with a crazed stalker? Her knees were shaking badly as she tiptoed to the open closet door and peered inside. Everything that had been hanging was piled on the floor, making it easy to see inside the empty space. Thank goodness no one was waiting to kill her.

Her legs refused to hold her up any longer, but she made it to the bed before collapsing. Stomach rolling and heart racing, she fought pure panic. She started to shake, her whole body as cold as a glacier.

Wrapping herself in a blanket, she rocked back and forth until the spots before her eyes finally disappeared. *Think.* She needed to regain some kind of calm and think.

The rest of the house had seemed fine. No sign of anything out of place. So all this hatred and evil had been directed at her.

But who in Chance would hate her enough to…?

The answer hit her and splattered her to pieces like a truck barreling down the highway. It had to have been *him!* In fact, all the sabotage on the ranch had to have been coming from him, too.

Her target, the second man she'd come to Chance to find, had found her first.

Chapter 14

"*Damn*," the man standing in a shadow below Summer's room muttered under his breath. It had taken the bitch nearly the whole morning to finally show up back in her room to find what he'd done.

She sure was pretty. Pretty enough to want to eat. Though slow on the uptake.

But he bet she got his message now. He'd caught a glimpse of the terror on her face when she'd come to the window.

That ought to take Travis Chance down a peg or two. The bastard was so smug. Just sure that he could protect his own and track down all enemies without breaking a sweat. Wrong guess, Chance.

The owner of the Bar-C hadn't even been able to find his enemy when he'd been right under his nose. Ha!

Eenie, meenie, minnie, moe. Catch a tiger by the toe. If he eats you, let him go!

Rubbing his hands together and finding them to be both sweaty and cold, the man tried to organize his thoughts. He needed to feel sure everything was in place for his plan to come together. But he was positive he'd been thorough and smart enough to set the trap correctly.

Yes, indeed. Come to papa, you crazy broad. You're gonna make terrific bait.

His major plan was just getting to the good part. Too bad the woman would have to die.

Chapter 15

Summer couldn't get out of the guest room fast enough. It took her two minutes to find clean underwear, jeans and a shirt. Sixty more seconds to put them on and run her hands through her hair to comb out the tangles.

By the time she made it to the kitchen, she was out of breath. But she ran to the ranch intercom and dialed the office. One of the hands answered and said he'd be right there.

Pacing the kitchen floor while she waited, it suddenly hit her that the man who was after her could be working for Travis. What a terrible thought. She hadn't met everyone who worked on the Bar-C yet. Of course he could work here.

She started to shake again as she ran to the drawer and pulled one of the butcher knives out of the block. Holding it made her feel a little better, but not a lot.

Was it too late to run? A banging on the back door gave her an answer.

"Ms. Wheeler, it's Billy Ray and Charlie. Let us in."

Two men had come? Gasping for air, she realized she'd been holding her breath. At least one of these men would help her, even if the other was her stalker.

She unlocked and ripped open the back door, and two strangers were in the mudroom before she had time to be afraid. But to her relief, both hands were strangers and entered the house quickly and carefully.

"Upstairs in the guest room," she managed in a too-high voice.

One of the men carefully locked the kitchen door behind him and then joined the other. "I'll check upstairs, Charlie. You make sure everything is locked down tight on the first floor."

Summer stood out of the way for a few seconds, put the knife back, and then crept up the stairs to see what was going on. Billy Ray was checking every room and every closet. He also jiggled every window lock, just to make sure.

"Which room?" he asked when he returned to the hall from Jenna's room.

Unable to speak, she pointed at the guest bedroom.

"Stay out here in the hall," Billy Ray told her as he opened the door and stepped inside.

Nodding absently, she followed him.

After checking the closet, he went straight to the balcony door and tried it. "Was this locked?"

"Not when I first came in this morning."

"Did you lock it last night?"

"I don't remember. But it's two stories up. How…?"

Unlocking the door, Billy Ray checked outside and then inspected the lock. "Could've had a ladder. It's not that high. And the door looks like it could've been jimmied. When did this happen?"

"Um…I can't be sure."

"So, do you think the guy could've done all this damage while you were asleep right in the same room?"

She didn't want to embarrass Travis by saying that she hadn't slept in this room for most of the night last night. And truthfully, she hadn't bothered to turn the light on when she gotten up at 1:00 a.m., so it was possible she had actually been here while it happened.

"Maybe."

Billy Ray threw her an incredulous look that said he thought she might be crazy. He could join the rest of the town.

All of a sudden, she just wanted these men gone. Out of the house. "If you'll check the rest of the house and then around the grounds, I'll clean this up."

"Don't you think Travis needs to see the mess?"

"Not especially. I can tell him about it."

Billy Ray shrugged. "Okay. Then why don't I call him or Barrett? One of them should get back here."

"That's not necessary. They're busy in town with Travis's brother Gage, but they'll be back soon enough."

"Ma'am." He nodded as if he accepted her word but then narrowed his eyes at her. "You shouldn't be in the house alone, you know. You want one of us to stay with you?"

"No, thanks. I intend to go to town, too. Just as soon as I clean the room."

He stood with an indecisive look on his face. She knew he wanted to stay with her, but he also didn't want to offend a woman who might be his boss's girlfriend.

Travis's girlfriend. Instead of the good feelings those words should've produced when she'd thought them, they just made her nauseous.

It was past time to take a stand. She had to find her

quarry and put a stop to all this—before Travis or Jenna really got hurt as innocent bystanders. She was obviously the cause of all the trouble. But she still needed help to track down her target, the stalker. She couldn't find a man as elusive as this one on her own. He'd already proven he was tricky. And dangerous.

"Look," she said on a sigh. "You and your buddy finish checking around the house, and then come back to nail the upstairs balcony doors and windows shut. Just until Travis's brother can come do a better security job. When you're finished, I'll go to town and see if I can catch Gage. I'll make sure he'll be out here later this evening to do a more professional job."

Billy Ray lifted his hat so he could scratch his head. She knew that meant he was thinking things over. She'd heard Travis tell him to do whatever she asked. Her guess was he'd do what she told him, even if he didn't think it was a smart idea.

"Yes, ma'am."

As soon as he was out of the room, she zipped around, shoving clothes in her duffel and straightening the drawers and bed linens. There wasn't anything she could do about the destroyed pillows or pictures, but she dumped them in the trash and then vacuumed up the rest of the mess.

While she worked, she formulated a plan. She would write Travis a note of explanation that she could mail later, then go pick up her car from the garage. Her old Ford must be close to ready by now. After doing that, she'd stop in to ask Gage for help. She'd earned enough now to be able to afford a motel in the next county over, and that's where she would go until she and Gage could find her man.

It wasn't safe for Travis or Jenna if she stayed on the ranch any longer. Besides, she couldn't bear watching

Travis's face when he learned the truth that she'd been keeping from him all this time. It would kill her to see him in such emotional pain.

But he was bound to be in pain one way or the other. It didn't matter if she stayed or left. Better for everyone involved if he wasn't put into a corner, with no choice but to demand she leave the ranch so he could protect his daughter. She knew that would kill him, too.

Summer tried to write her letter while the men nailed the second-story balcony doors shut. But she only managed to wad up enough paper to fill an entire trash can.

Knowing someone on the ranch was bound to call Travis or Barrett soon and tell them what had happened, she gave up and decided to try again later to write the letter. Right now she needed to hurry up and leave the ranch—before something else much worse happened.

Travis, along with his foreman, Barrett, faced his brother's back as Gage finalized security plans for the ranch house and immediate vicinity on the computer. "What'll it take to get this all done? And how fast can you do the job?" he demanded.

"You should've taken care of this years ago," Gage muttered over his shoulder. "Or at the latest, when Sam and Grace were having all that trouble last spring. I can pick up the equipment in the next few days and install it as soon as I clear my calendar."

"Clear your calendar now. I'll fly you wherever you need to go to pick up equipment—but it'll be this afternoon. Someone's going to be hurt bad if we don't do something about this bastard today. And I'm danged determined it won't be Jenna or Summer."

Gage gave him a funny look. "What is it with you and Summer?"

"None of your business." Rather than let his brother's remark rile him, he went on. "Barrett and I will begin putting in place the plan you suggested to unmask the culprit. We'll start talking to each of the hands and watch how they react. You're right. Someone with easy access to the ranch, like one of the hands, has to be our guy."

Gage nodded, but before he could add anything else, Barrett's cell phone rang and the foreman had to excuse himself to take the call.

"You're absolutely positive that Barrett's not our man?" Gage asked when the other man was out of hearing range.

"Positive. Half the time when things have happened, Barrett's either been with me or he's been off the ranch running errands. He didn't have opportunity. Plus, he doesn't have a motive. Barrett's been well taken care of and could buy his own spread if he wanted to. He's always claimed he'd rather stay on the Bar-C where he feels at home."

"Boss." Barrett opened the door and came back into Gage's office. "That call was one of the hands I'd left to watch over the house. There's been another incident. Seems our saboteur turned into a second-story man and managed to access the guest room where Ms. Summer's been staying. Made one holy mess of the place."

"What! Is Summer all right?" His mind blanked and, through a fog of adrenaline, he couldn't think what he should do next.

He wanted to run. Or yell and shout. Or kill someone with his bare hands. But all he could do was stand there and let the disabling rush of hormones subside.

"She's fine," Barrett said. "Told the hands to nail the balcony doors and upstairs windows shut until Gage could do a better security job."

"I've got to get back." He turned to Gage, but was at a loss for words.

"Go. Call me and let me know what you need me to do."

"Uh, boss—" Barrett gained his attention again. "Billy Ray said she told him she was heading into town. You want to stay and wait for her? I'll go on back and check things out."

"No." He didn't know why, but he was sure he needed to be on Bar-C land as soon as possible. "Let's go. We should be able to catch her on the road to town. And if we miss her, she'll be better off here with Gage."

Barrett nodded, lifted his hand to Gage in goodbye and left.

Turning back to his brother, Travis said, "If she shows up here, call me. And then keep her safe while we question everyone. Jenna's already off the ranch for the weekend. I want Summer safely away. Maybe she can stay with Aunt June, too."

"You think we should get the sheriff involved?" Gage asked. "Things are out of control."

"No. I'm still not convinced the sheriff doesn't have something to do with all this. He's had a grudge against the Chance family ever since he had to arrest Dad for Mom's murder."

Gage nodded. "Yeah, and I probably didn't make that situation any better when I accused him of manufacturing evidence in order to get Dad out of the way. Frankly, I'm still not sure that Dad and the sheriff didn't have some private beef going on back then."

Travis nodded absently, too concerned with what was happening on the ranch to pay close attention. "Listen, I'm gone. If Summer shows up, call me."

"I will. And I'll get the equipment ordered. We'll stop this creep, Trav."

"You bet we will. No one screws with the Bar-C and people I care about. No one." He turned and, following Barrett down the stairs, walked back out to his truck.

As he went, his mind whirled with possibilities. Men he knew that might want to harm the ranch or him personally.

Gage had been wrong. Things weren't out of control. Not yet. He had only just begun to make things right.

Summer pulled the SUV into Stockard's parking lot with her eyes welling up. Now that she'd made the decision to go, she was having trouble staying the course she'd set. What about Jenna? Having to leave the little girl behind was an impossible situation. If she stayed on the Bar-C, Jenna wouldn't be safe. But how could she walk away from the motherless child she'd begun to love as if she was her own?

A smiling Jimmy Stockard came out to greet her and leaned in to talk when she rolled down the window. "Morning, Summer."

"Hi, Jimmy. I don't see my car. Is it all fixed?"

An odd look crossed his face as he sobered in a hurry. "Uh, no, not yet."

"Really? But you said a couple of weeks, and it's that now. What happened?"

Screwing up his mouth in a frown, Jimmy took a deep breath. "Look, I don't want to get into any trouble with Travis. But I'm not good at telling stories."

"Telling stories? What stories? Is my car okay?"

"Well," Jimmy began hesitantly, "Travis asked me to put off fixing your car, but he didn't want you to know it was his idea. He said to make up a story about lost parts that sounded believable. But that sort of thing just ain't my style."

"Travis said that? But why? Why would he do such a thing?"

"He didn't say why, but I can guess." He gave her a pointed look. "Can't you?"

"No. Travis Chance is the most honest man I've ever met. Why would he want you to lie?"

"Aw, come on, Summer. It's not like that's a real hurtful lie. The man is crazy about you. You can see it in his eyes when he mentions your name. I'm guessing he's only finding excuses to get you to stay."

She opened her mouth to say something, but couldn't think of a thing that would make any sense. And certainly nothing that she would want to say to Jimmy.

Her first emotion had been anger over Travis trying to control the situation again. But after a second she knew her feelings were much more complicated than that.

She wanted to stay, too. More than she'd considered. And if it were just her safety she had to consider, she *would* stay. Maybe forever, if she could talk him into it. But it wasn't just her safety on the line. It was Travis and Jenna's lives that mattered the most now.

Jimmy looked terrified that she hadn't said a word. She decided to at least let him off the hook.

"It's okay," she murmured. "I won't mention that you told me the truth. Travis doesn't need to know."

But now she had a bigger problem. She couldn't take a Bar-C SUV and leave town. Someone might accuse her of stealing it.

Darn. Her life was turning into one big, confusing and potentially dangerous puzzle.

And she'd brought every single bad thing down around her shoulders all by herself.

Gage had to be her next stop. He hadn't been all that friendly when she'd met him the first time. But she was positive he loved his brother. He would help her because of Travis.

She asked Jimmy for directions to Gage's office and then bid him goodbye. The mechanic looked relieved to see her go. She certainly wasn't making many friends in this town. Leaving would be for the best—in several ways. Except for Jenna. Jenna was the innocent bystander in all of this.

After making her way across town and parking behind a two-story building, Summer climbed the stairs to Gage's office on the second floor. When she entered his office, she found him sitting in front of a bank of computers, concentrating on one screen.

He turned his head when he heard the door close behind her. "Oh, it's you, Summer. Been expecting you. Hang on a second, I'm almost finished here."

He'd been expecting her? A sudden chill rode down her arms. But after a second to take a breath, she calmed down and remembered Travis had been here visiting Gage earlier this morning. Maybe one of the ranch hands had called looking for him.

Gage punched another combination of buttons on the computer and turned to fully face her. "Sorry you missed Travis on the road. Better he explain things to you than me. But…so be it."

"Explain what?" Now she was confused again.

"Travis has decided to go to war against his stalker."

"W…war? What does that mean?"

"He's taking steps to stop the jerk for good. Steps like arming the hands he's sure he can trust. In fact, right about now he should be putting everyone on the Bar-C through an interrogation so he can be assured of who is on his side.

And I'll be installing extra security around the barns and house. If anyone messes with the Bar-C after that, he'll be sorry."

"But…but people can get hurt during a war."

"Yes, ma'am. And that's why Travis wants you and Jenna to stay off the ranch for a while. Just until we figure out who's been doing these things."

This had gotten totally out of hand. No one could be hurt or worse because of her. She could never live with herself afterward—no matter where she went. Nowhere on earth would be far enough away to ever give her any peace.

"But I know who's been doing it," she blurted out.

Gage gave her a look she hoped to never see again on anyone's face. "What do you know? Who is it?" His mouth was narrowed to a dangerous line, and his hazel eyes were dark and glaring.

"No, please listen, Gage. It's a long story. I was coming here to ask you for help."

"Before you told Travis what you know? Not very loyal, are you, woman?"

How had she managed to get herself into such a mess? "Just give me a chance to explain. I'm the one that brought all the trouble to the Bar-C. It's me he's after."

Gage moved fast. He jumped up and grabbed her by the shoulders. Shoving her roughly into a chair, he kept one hand biting into her shoulder to make sure she stayed put.

"Don't move." He pointed his finger at her as if it was a gun. "Say your piece, but hurry it up. You have ten minutes to convince me not to turn you over to the sheriff."

Chapter 16

"And that's the whole story." Summer rushed ahead, completely out of breath. "When I saw what he'd written on the mirror in the guest room, I knew the stalker was after me. I'm the target. Not Travis or the Bar-C. I can't stand by and see anyone else get hurt." Especially not the man she loved or his daughter.

"So you've been lying to Travis." Gage was still glaring, but he'd taken a step backward to scrutinize her and her words. "And staying with him under false pretenses. You do realize my brother has fallen in love with you, don't you? What the hell were you going to do about that?"

"He's never said he loved me." Now she was being ridiculous. Of course she knew he loved her. That's what had been slowing killing her all this time.

Gage threw her another threatening look and reached for the phone.

"Wait. Yes, I know he loves me. I'm in love with him,

too. But he's too good a man for me, Gage. He'd be a lot better off without me."

"Agree with you there. But I don't count. Travis has to make that decision."

"Please help me find the stalker first," she begged. "I know what he looks like. And I'm sure he has to be either on the ranch or somewhere nearby."

Gage finally collapsed back down in his chair. "I guess you haven't done anything technically illegal. Immoral, yes. But there's no sense involving the sheriff in our problems."

"Thank you. Thank you. Travis isn't too crazy about this sheriff, and I was hesitant to drag him into anything until I knew where the stalker was for certain."

"Right." Gage waved off her thanks. "Tell me again what this guy looks like and how long he's supposedly been in our area." He turned to his computer and typed in a couple of things.

She did her best to describe the very average-looking guy she would never forget. Then she said, "And the P.I. I hired said he'd heard the man had been back here in the Chance vicinity for at least a couple of years."

"Hmm. Shouldn't be too hard to find someone who was raised around here and left town only to return recently. You say he's supposedly around age fifty?"

"He looked younger than that to me, but the P.I. said that's what he'd found out when he located an informant who'd been buddies with the guy in prison."

"Why didn't you give all this information to the police and let them handle it?"

Exasperated, she blew out a breath. "Are you going to help me find him? Is that what all these questions are about?"

Gage frowned but looked at her with a change of

attitude. But she couldn't tell what he was thinking. Nevertheless, his expression made her nervous.

"I did tell the police everything I found out," she said with something like a whine in her voice. "They took a report, but they never did anything. I got tired of waiting."

More than tired. This quest to find Hoss had become the only thing keeping her out of the depths of depression. And out of an institution. And alive.

Until she'd met Travis.

"I'll help you find him," Gage agreed. "Shouldn't be too hard."

She felt her shoulders relaxing as the air in her lungs whooshed out in relief. "Oh, thank…"

Gage raised his hand, palm out, to make her stop talking. "But first you have to tell Travis the truth. Every bit of it. I'm not doing a thing until he gives the okay. And if he decides he'd rather just run you out of town, I'll be the first to give you a shove."

Her back straightened and she looked down at her hands. "I guess I deserve that. I brought the danger right to his door."

"Fine." Gage reached for the phone. "Sit right there and tell him now. Get it over with."

"Wait!" She felt the panic rise up in her chest and threaten to choke her. "I can't. I can't tell him over the phone. I need to see him in person. This is too…personal…for a phone call."

Gage's hand hovered over the phone's receiver. "It's personal, all right. It's going to hurt him to hear the truth." Gage rubbed at his own chest as if the thought of hurting his brother hurt him, too.

From that moment, Summer knew she was going to

like this man. No matter that he hated her. Anyone who loved Travis so deeply was a friend of hers.

"I'll find a way to break it to him easy, Gage. I swear. But I have to see his face when I do. Surely you can understand that."

Dropping his hand, Gage took a deep breath. "You're right. You owe it to him to face his anger head-on. I'll call him and tell him to come back to the office."

"But I thought telling him on the ranch would be better. Easier for him. I'll go back now." She stood and turned to the door.

"Hold it." Gage reached again for the phone. "You stay right there. Travis wanted you out of the danger."

Yes, that sounded like something Travis would say. But as Gage raised the ranch and waited for Travis to come to the phone, she eased herself toward the door.

She couldn't tell Travis the truth as long as his brother was looking over their shoulders. It was bound to embarrass Travis, and she couldn't say all the words she'd wanted to tell him.

No, much better if she told him alone. In person. While he was standing on the ranch he loved so much. Just as Gage said hello, she slid out the door and made a run for the SUV.

Hold on, Travis. I'm coming to tell you something terrible. Wait for me. You'll know the truth soon enough.

She made it out of town in record time and without anyone following. She'd worried about the sheriff spotting her speeding and trying to stop her. But she needn't have worried. No one seemed to be around on this quiet autumn afternoon in Chance.

Once outside the town limits and back on Bar-C land, she relaxed. Gage wouldn't come after her now. And if

Travis came from the other direction, toward town, to meet her, they were bound to run into each other. Talking to him out here on the range might be just as well. It was certainly private, with miles and miles of empty ranch land as far as the eye could see.

Going over in her head what she would say, she tried every angle to put her lies in the best light. But as she traveled past brown grass pastures and crossed over cattle guards with their eerie clanking sounds, she finally came to the conclusion that there was no way to put a lie in a good light.

Travis was going to be furious, and he had every right to be mad. She'd brought danger into his world and hadn't even given him the opportunity to prepare or defend his family and his home.

Would he end up hating her? Her only saving grace was that she loved him and would do anything to make things right in the end. Whatever he asked of her—to leave Chance and never come back or to stay nearby and spend as much time with Jenna as he would allow. Whatever he wanted, she would be willing. Gladly. But nothing would ever be the same between them.

Lost in her contemplations as she crossed a bridge over a gully, she almost didn't notice a pickup nose-down among the hackberries and mesquite. She slammed on the brakes and backed up to look closer.

Was that a body in the driver's seat? The coming dusk made shadows under the trees, and she couldn't tell from this distance. But it did seem as though somebody had lost control and accidentally slid their truck into the gully.

Someone could be hurt. She made a too-quick decision to check things out and see if she could be of help. Driving her SUV over brushy land to get a closer look, she came up on the truck and realized its color was white. The same as the pickup she'd been looking for since she'd come to town. But there wasn't any red writing on the side. No writing of any kind at all. Still, this truck looked familiar.

Ignoring the warning bells going off in the back of her mind, she parked within ten yards and opened her door. Before she stepped out, she checked the whole area to be sure no one else was anywhere nearby.

Her nerves were jangling and blood was pounding in her ears. But her deep desire to help a person in need overtook her better judgment and blinded her to even normal wariness. Maybe she should just tiptoe closer to get a better look.

Hoping to make herself invisible, she stayed low until she was right next to the pickup's bed. She flattened herself against it and inched her way to the driver's window.

When she got within a foot, she could hear moaning. Someone *was* hurt.

Throwing all caution and care to the winds, she grabbed hold of the door handle and ripped open the door. A man was bent over the steering wheel and groaning as though he was hurt badly. Right away she knew he wasn't her quarry. Even from the side, she could tell this man was much younger than the man she'd been looking for.

"Where does it hurt?" Leaning in, she tried to put her arm around his shoulders to help him sit up, but his back was too wide.

The man moaned as she took hold of his arm, and she caught a whiff of alcohol. No wonder he'd run off the road. He must be drunk.

"I don't have a cell phone to call for help," she said in a raised voice. "Do you have a phone? I can call the ranch to send help and get you out of here."

All of a sudden the man came to life and sat back,

swiveling his body to face her. "I'll do any calling," he growled.

Stunned, she took a half step back and realized this unshaven, untidy man was someone she'd seen before. She remembered going with Travis one Saturday to give this creepy fellow charitable assistance. His name was Bodie something, as she recalled. Travis had offered him a job.

She opened her mouth to ask what he thought he was doing when she belatedly noticed he had a gun pointed directly at her belly button.

"Whaaa…?" That was all she could manage, as her voice stuck in her throat.

"Shut up, bitch. I'll do the talking, too." He climbed out of the pickup but kept the gun barrel directed squarely toward the center of her chest.

"You really are slow on the uptake, you know that? But you're going to be moving fast from here on out. I have things to do, and you are going to behave so I can get them done in time. Understand?"

Her brain wasn't functioning. What had he said?

He slapped her hard across the cheek. "Wake up, you dumb broad. Pay attention."

She bit her lip to keep from crying out and tasted blood. What did he want with her?

"Don't move a muscle. You hear me? Not until I say so, or I'll shoot you where you stand."

He stuffed the gun in his waistband and reached back to bring out a piece of rope from behind the front seat. She thought for about one second about trying to run, then decided he would just shoot her in the back before she got very far.

After tying her hands behind her, he roughly grabbed her by the arm and dragged her around to the other side of the truck. "Get in. And hurry it up."

Having her hands tied was too much like the worst night of her life. The horror of her past closed in, surrounding her with creeping terrors. Shifting memories of dark shadows and echoes of footsteps on the floor above her head weakened her knees and threatened to make her lose whatever was in her stomach.

Irritated by her slow movements, he picked her up around the waist, threw her in the front seat and slammed the door shut. "Damned bumbling bitch. Don't move."

Not moving was easy—she was frozen to the spot. But somewhere in the deep recesses of her mind she found a strength she didn't know she possessed. On that first terrible night long ago, she'd fought with everything she had inside to live so she could save her child. This time she would fight to stay alive because Travis had given her something to live for.

Somehow, someway, she would live through this night to see Travis once more.

Over her shoulder, she heard the Bar-C's SUV start up. Looking out the back window, she saw Bodie driving it right toward the deepest part of the gully. He gunned the engine and jumped free just as the SUV hit the slope. The SUV jerked and rolled, landing out of sight under the bridge.

She tried to breathe but couldn't seem to get enough air. What did this guy want?

Before she could think of any of the excruciating but quite possible answers to that question, he was back and climbing in the driver's seat. "That ought to do the job. We're out of here. There's more work to be done before we call your sweetheart."

What? "Travis? What do you want with him?"

Bodie gave her a quick, backhanded slap across the mouth. "I told you to shut the hell up."

He cranked the starter, and the pickup's engine roared to life. "Don't you worry, missy. You and our friend Trav will be seeing each other real soon." Laughing under his breath he added, "And spending time side by side—throughout eternity."

By the time Travis reached his brother's office, both his mind and his pickup were out of control. Slamming into the parking lot, he raced up the stairs and stormed down the hall.

He barged through the office door. "Where the devil is she? We didn't meet up on the road like you said we would."

"Calm down." Gage stood to face him. "I'm sure…"

"Calm, hell! How could you let her leave?"

"Let her? She sneaked out when my back was turned. I told her to talk to you on the phone. It was all her big idea that she had to tell you in person."

With his brain racing and adrenaline gushing through his veins, Travis did something really stupid. He took both hands and shoved Gage hard in the chest.

The minute he'd done it, he regretted the move. But he was already up to his ears in horse manure and couldn't seem to get a handle on his self-control.

Gage balled his fists but stood his ground. "No sense taking it out on me, brother. I was just looking after your interests."

"Then you tell me what was so all-fired important that she had to drive out to the ranch when I told you to keep her here and safe."

Gage turned his back and walked to the window. Smart move. His brother knew damned well he would never attack a man from behind.

"Well?" He balled his own fists and stuck them in his pockets.

"You'd really rather hear this from her. But looks like I've got no choice. Summer knows who the stalker is."

"What?" His ears were ringing, and the dusky light coming through the window grew dimmer.

Gage swung back around. "Better sit to hear this."

"Hell, no. Get on with it."

"She's been living on the ranch through false pretenses, Trav. Using you to get what she came to town for. You are such an easy touch. If I've told you…"

Travis stumbled forward but stopped short of putting his hands around Gage's neck and wringing the story out of him. "Just tell me what she said."

Gage backed up a step and put his chin up. "She came to Chance deliberately—looking for the man who got away from the scene when her family was murdered. Looking for final justice, she claimed. Seemed the cops wouldn't help, so she hired a P.I. to track him down, but she doesn't know what name he's been using. She got a good look at him the night of the murders. And she's been searching for him since the day she got here."

Shaking his head, Travis tried to make some sense of what Gage was saying. "Why didn't she tell me? Why keep it a secret?"

Gage shrugged a shoulder. "That part was kinda vague. Something about starting off with a lie and not knowing how to stop."

"But… Why does she think the ranch's stalker is this man she's looking for?"

"Well, that's more complicated, I think. She spotted the guy in town a while back and is sure he got a good look at her, too. Then, when her room was trashed, apparently the stalker wrote something like 'Die, bitch' on the mirror. She's convinced that means it's someone who's specifically after her."

Travis backed into a desk chair and plopped down. He couldn't make his mind settle enough to think this through.

"Why come to you?" he finally asked. "Why not confess to me and let me handle things?"

Gage lowered his voice, sounding calm, as though he was trying to be solicitous. "That's the worst of it. She was on her way out of town. Running from the danger. Came to me because she thought another P.I. could track the guy down and stop him from coming after her."

"Running?" His brain refused to process the words. "Leaving without talking to me first? Without explaining to Jenna?"

"I'm sorry, Trav. I didn't want to be the one to tell you. I asked her to wait for you, and then I thought maybe she'd gone to the ranch to tell you in private. But since you didn't meet up on the road—I'm thinking she decided to run after all."

Getting to his feet, Travis set his jaw and turned in a circle, trying to focus. "I don't buy it."

"Look at the facts." Gage held his palms out and pleaded with his eyes. "Wake up and see her for what she really is."

"What she really is—a woman who's changed my whole world." And she was so much more. "She's a survivor. A woman who lived through the worst thing a parent could ever live through. She found a way into my daughter's heart—and mine too, when I was damned sure I would never love any woman again."

The tears welled in his eyes. "I trust her, Gage. With everything in me. She didn't just run. She came to you for help. And if she said she was coming to tell me the truth, then something awful stopped her first."

"Trav…"

"We've got to find her." Belatedly regaining control of his mind, he made a mental list of things a search party could do. "I'll call Barrett and head back out to the ranch. You call the sheriff. It's time to get him involved." As he reached the door, his cell phone rang.

Hanging back, he answered the anonymous call. "Travis Chance."

"I've got the bitch, Chance." The voice was garbled, deliberately disguised. "So far she's okay. But if you don't do what I say, you'll never see her again."

Travis blanked his mind to the terror in the words. He'd come to his senses and needed to remain strong.

"This is the worst joke I've ever heard. Your script sounds like a bad television show. You're not funny. If you've got Summer, put her on."

"Shut up and listen, bastard. You know I've got her. I've been able to move around everywhere on the ranch, including inside the ranch house, and you haven't been able to stop me. This is all on your head, Travis Chance. Either do as I say or be the cause of her death."

"What do you want?"

Silence from the other end gave Travis chills clear down to his bones. He felt sure the other man didn't have anything specific in mind. That he'd only wanted to cause pain. And he was doing a damned good job of it. But Travis waited him out.

Finally the disguised voice gave him instructions. Wanting money and a plane seemed like another cliché. But Travis agreed readily.

Summer had to be alive. And he was going to see to it that she stayed that way.

After the man hung up, Travis turned to his brother. "She's been kidnapped. The stalker wants money and a plane ride. I'll take care of those. You call the sheriff. But I want it understood that I'm in charge. No one makes any moves that could get her killed. Understand?"

"How much time do we have?"

"Two hours." Not nearly enough for a decent plan.

Yet every second was too damned long. In one way, the kidnapper was right. Travis should've never let Summer out of his sight. This was all on him.

Chapter 17

"What are you doing?" Summer's hands and feet were numb, and she could barely see her kidnapper through the growing darkness.

"Shut up." He'd been diligently working on some project since they'd arrived at a broken-down shack near the Bar-C's airstrip. "If I want you to know anything, I'll tell you."

For the second time in her life, she felt sure she was about to die. *Snap out of it,* she chided herself. She would be no help to Travis if she was too scared to think. And Travis's welfare was all that mattered anymore.

Her life was probably over. She'd overheard Bodie's ransom call to Travis but had developed a growing suspicion that her captor had no intention of letting her live after he got what he wanted.

Come to think of it, that was another thing that didn't feel right. What did he really want? Not money. She felt sure money was the last thing on his mind.

Bodie was mumbling to himself, as he had been over the last hour. He sat at a rickety table with a flashlight in one hand and worked at some small piece of equipment on the table.

"Right. Right," he muttered to himself. "I remember, Daddy. Oww. Don't hit me again. I'll do it proper." He jerked his head as though something hard had smacked him across the cheek.

Oh, dear Lord, the man was losing it. Those were the first clear words she'd understood, and now she had to fight a bad case of panic. He was hearing voices. That couldn't be a good sign.

Tugging fruitlessly against the ropes on her wrists, she thought back to another night when she'd been in a similar spot. But that time the ropes had seemed looser—easier to slip off. The dark memories of that night haunted her. But now she had to wonder. Had Hoss deliberately left her ties loose, knowing she would have a chance to set herself free?

On that night long ago, she'd failed to save her child, the only thing that had mattered in her world. But tonight, she vowed, would be different. If she had any strength left—or a tiny shot at all of foiling this guy's plans—she intended to die before letting him kill Travis.

"There we go," Bodie said with pride in his voice. "Almost all set for the final act."

He stood and walked over to her spot on the floor in a dark corner. "Your boyfriend's due in another few minutes and we're nearly ready for him."

Squatting on his haunches, he folded his hands and leered at her. "Too bad things must turn out this way. I'd have liked an opportunity to see how good you are in bed. Travis sure seemed to enjoy it."

"You've been spying on us?"

"Stupid, stupid bitch. I've been more than spying. I've been running things on the Bar-C for the last month. How'd you enjoy your first horseback ride? Exciting enough for you?"

"But why? Why all the dirty tricks? Someone could've been killed."

She saw right away from the look on his face that he wouldn't mind if anyone was hurt or killed. His lack of concern for life chilled her as if it were a cold stake driven through her heart. He expected someone to die tonight.

Shaking his head, he rolled his eyes as though she was the most naive person he'd ever met. "Payback. You should know how that feels. I'll bet you've had your share of thoughts on a payback of your own over the last few years. Ain't that right?"

Opening her mouth to deny his accusation, she stopped short. Yes, she'd admit to a few daydreams of taking retribution for the wrongs done to her and her child. But they'd only been fleeting thoughts. Gone before she'd really recognized the pain behind them.

"Not payback," she insisted. "I don't want anyone else hurt. I just want justice."

"Justice?" Bodie grinned, looking crazier than ever. "Now ain't that a high-and-mighty word. I like it. Yessir. That's what I'll be doing tonight. Getting justice for all the years of being nothing but chicken turds under Travis Chance's boot."

She caught it then. The real reason for everything he'd done. He planned on killing Travis tonight. And she was the bait for his plan.

"You won't get away if you hurt Travis. You'll go to jail. You don't want that, do you?"

He shrugged, almost nonchalantly. "Don't plan on getting away. Don't plan on going back to jail, either."

Straightening up, he went to the table and picked up the thing he'd been working on. "Nope. Tonight we're going to have enough fun to last a lifetime."

He pocketed whatever he'd picked up, then reached for a bottle sitting on the other end of the table. "Let's have us a little drink to celebrate justice, then I need to finish up. We're expecting our guest soon." Hoisting the bottle in one hand, he took a long swig but didn't offer her any.

Suicide. Horrified, her mind began taking in all she'd heard and seen. She would bet that was some kind of bomb he'd been making.

Bodie didn't plan on using a plane or spending the money. He expected to die. And he planned on taking her and Travis with him when he did.

It was everything Travis could do to keep from stomping his foot on the accelerator. Nice and easy does it. He was leading a small parade of trucks toward the airstrip with his headlights off.

He'd had a hell of a time convincing Sheriff McCord and his brother to let him take the money to the meeting spot alone. But that's what the kidnapper had ordered, and that's the way things would go. Travis refused to take any chances with Summer's life.

He'd finally agreed to let the sheriff set up a perimeter around an abandoned line-shack near the end of the runway. Still, Travis had insisted everyone move into position without lights. No truck lights. No flashlights. Nothing that would give them away. He relented only on the point of allowing runway lights and running lights for the Cessna. The kidnapper had ordered the plane, and they would need enough light to see the situation.

The closer he came to the airstrip, the more he wondered who it was they were really dealing with. He'd been born and raised in Chance County, Texas, and was sure he knew every single soul who'd ever lived here. So, who really was this guy named Hoss?

Every time he tried to focus on her man, though, he kept circling around to their stalker. He just didn't see how or why the man Summer was seeking, a coward who had run away, could be the one who'd set up all the so-called accidents on the Bar-C. In his gut, Travis was still positive that he had been the stalker's target. The things the guy had done were far too personal and seemed directed solely at him.

Even trashing Summer's room and scaring her had felt like a strike aimed at him and not her. It was almost as if the stalker had been shouting, in loud and clear tones, that he was every bit as powerful as Travis and could do whatever he wanted, whenever he wanted.

Just then they arrived at a spot behind the hangar where they'd planned to split up. Travis cleared his mind, put the pickup in neutral, and got out to direct the others to their spots.

The sheriff was the first to meet him. "You've only got ten minutes, Chance. Do you have the money?"

"It's in the truck. And the plane should already be in place. You and the men need to move to your positions now. But I don't want anyone shooting at anything unless they see I've been incapacitated. Is that understood?"

"I heard you over the phone the first time." The sheriff carried a high-powered rifle with a night scope in the crook of his arm. "Gage has outfitted all of us with communications equipment. Let him wire you before you head out. That way, if we can't see you, at least we can hear what's going on."

Travis had been clear about his wishes. No wires. No

guns. Nothing that could be seen as threatening to the kidnapper.

"Not for me. You don't need to hear what I'm saying. The only time you should order any action is if I'm laid out on the ground. Got that?"

The sheriff nodded but didn't look happy.

Gage came up to them at that moment. "Ready, brother?"

"As ready as I'll ever be. I just wish I knew who I was going to be facing. Watch my back." He turned to the pickup.

Gage snagged his arm. "Wait." He thrust a .38 semi-automatic into his hand. "Conceal this under your shirt. Take it, Travis. Don't go alone and unarmed."

Shaking his head, he handed the weapon back to Gage. "I'm not taking any chances with her life. I can't. If she dies due to something I did wrong, I'll never live with myself."

"But you haven't put her in this position. She got there all by herself. Being in love is one thing, but don't be foolish."

Travis had nothing to say to Gage. His brother had thought he'd been in love once, and it had not worked out well—somewhat the same as Travis's own experience with his ex-wife. But since Summer had come into his life, Travis had changed his mind about love. Everything appeared in a different light when you actually found the right person.

"Go get into position," he told Gage as he climbed into the pickup and turned on the headlights.

Driving out on the tarmac, he headed down the runway toward the old shack. He told himself to put Summer out of his mind—that thinking of her could slow down his response time when dealing with the kidnapper.

But immediately he saw that any such thing would be impossible. His whole life revolved around her now. This confrontation was all about her, at least in his mind, if not the kidnapper's.

No, he didn't mind dying for her sake, if that's what it took. But to his last breath, he'd be devoted to seeing her get out of this alive.

"Well, your boyfriend is right on time for the party." Bodie laughed as though that was the funniest joke that had ever been told.

They'd heard the small plane pulling up on the runway close by a few minutes ago, and since then Bodie had been staring out the window, around the newspapers covering the glass. Now she could also make out the sounds of a pickup. Travis was here.

Summer promised herself she'd think of something to do to warn him. She couldn't just sit and let everything go this crazy man's way.

But, drunk as he seemed to be, Bodie was smart enough to guess her thoughts. "Nothing you can do to prevent what's ahead, missy. Start praying that you can endure pain well. Or that you pass out from the pain and are unconscious through the worst of it. As for me, I'm looking forward to what's coming."

He wasn't even drunk. But he was definitely insane.

"Why?" she whispered.

"Oh? Does that interest you? Maybe I'll keep you alive long enough to hear what a jerk your boyfriend has always been."

Through the shadowed darkness, she watched him stuffing a couple of things into his pockets. Then he picked up a huge hunting knife and stalked in her direction.

"I'd really like to rearrange your face a bit, just to torment Travis. But I can't figure out a way to make that work out with my plans." He chuckled as he sliced the knife through the ropes at her ankles.

He grabbed hold of her by the shoulder, ripped her off her bottom and jerked her to her feet. She heard an odd popping sound when he lifted her and felt excruciating pain in that shoulder. But she refused to cry out. She had to think past the pain.

"Now listen to me, bitch," he began as he produced a handgun. "You keep your mouth shut and do whatever I tell you, or I swear I will kill Travis right in front of your eyes. But first I'll make him suffer. One of my bullets at a time to one body part at a time."

She whimpered but kept her mouth shut. There had to be a way to stop this or warn Travis off.

"Aw, sorry for that image." He manhandled her toward the door. "You're not really the one I'm trying to hurt, you know. But if our friend reacts like I think he will, when he sees you being hurt, it'll kill him. Every twinge of pain you feel will be like a knife in his chest."

He opened the door carefully and then shoved her out in front of him. "Showtime."

Travis stared at the door to the shack, willing Summer to be all right. When she was pushed through it a second later, he heaved a huge sigh of relief. She was alive. That's all that mattered.

A man, still in the shadows, came out of the shack close behind her. Glints of light from the runway and plane gleamed off the weapon in the man's hand as he jammed the barrel into Summer's temple. Who was this guy?

Travis grabbed the duffel stuffed with money he'd stored behind the driver's seat and went forward to meet them. It had taken some doing to gather the money on such short notice, but he'd managed with Gage's help.

As he walked closer, the man stayed behind Summer, and Travis still couldn't make out who he was dealing with.

Until the next second, when the kidnapper spoke. "Took you long enough, Chance." *Bodie Barnes. But why?* "Bet you never guessed the identity of your stalker until right now, did you?"

Travis didn't bother to answer. But his mind kept sorting through loose facts. This could not be Summer's quarry. If Bodie had been the one all along, she would've recognized his face when she'd seen him the first time. So, Travis had been right. This stalking thing had been about him the whole time. And it still was.

"What are you after, Bodie?"

Travis searched Summer's face for some kind of expression that would tell him whether or not she was injured. But her face was a mask. All he could see was her fear.

The weapon in Bodie's hand suddenly pointed directly at him. And then the bastard gave Summer a little push out in front so he could partially hide himself behind her body. Her eyes grew wider.

"I'll ask the questions. Did you come alone like I told you?"

"Of course." Then, ignoring Bodie, he turned to Summer. "Are you all right?"

"Don't say nothing, bitch. Or he gets it."

Travis dropped the duffel at his feet and fisted his hands. "If you've touched one hair on her head, you're a dead man."

Bodie gave out an eerie belly laugh from where he

stood in the shadows. "There's nothing you can do, big man. I'm holding all the cards. Now, shut up and listen."

Travis kept his eyes trained on Summer, carefully watching her every move through the streaks of light coming from the runway. She was trembling and he could almost taste her fear.

"It's past time for you to know the way real pain feels," Bodie began in a high-pitched voice. "For years you've been dishing out hurt. Now it's your turn."

"I haven't done anything," Travis said through gritted teeth. "But I've got your money, and you can see the plane is right there. Take the duffel and go."

"I don't want your frigging money or your plane. I want you to listen to me for once."

Travis shut up, but he kept his eyes glued on Summer's face. This was not going to end well for someone. And it damned sure wouldn't be her.

"You murdered my father," Bodie whined. "Took away the only person who ever gave a damn whether I lived or died."

"He committed suicide," Travis corrected him. "Your father lived a tough life and couldn't get clean. I tried to help him and I had nothing to do with his death."

"Shut up!" Bodie's gun barrel went to Summer's neck. "I'm not the only one in town who feels this way. You and your family have done people wrong. There's a lot of hate built up against you. A couple of people have even been helping me. Egging me on. But they didn't have to."

"Travis…" Summer started to say something, but Bodie pointed the gun right back in his direction and she shut her mouth.

So, Bodie had probably threatened to kill him if she didn't cooperate. In that case, if he played this guy just right, maybe she had a real chance to live.

"Listen, pal." Travis tried to think fast on his feet. "You don't have to do this. There're places that can help you. Medicines that can take away the pain. Let me send you there. I can pay—"

"No one wants your tainted Chance money," Bodie screamed. "Can't you see that?"

Bodie made a rough sound like a growl and then lowered his voice. "No more talking. We're going to play us a little game. Let's see how much pain Travis Chance can stand to see inflicted on his little darling here."

"He's got a bomb in the cabin," Summer shouted.

Without any warning, Summer hiccupped and then collapsed in a silent heap at Bodie's feet. Horrified, Travis went toward her. "What the hell did you do to her?"

She began to twitch and moan as Bodie waved a gun in one hand and a Taser in the other. The man's eyes were wild as he pointed.

"Taser gun, man. It hurts like a son of a bitch. But she'll live if you stand back. Don't come any closer."

That was enough for Travis. He had a promise to keep, and Bodie had just hurt her for the first and last time.

But Bodie spoke before Travis could react. "Okay, Chance, you were right. Pick her up and carry her into the shack where we can see better."

From her position on the ground, Summer groaned up at him. "Noooo. The bomb."

Bodie cursed and bent down, reaching to grab hold of her hair. It was all the opening Travis needed. He sprang at the other man's gun hand, intending to knock the weapon away.

Several things happened at one time. The gun went off and a sharp pain shot through Travis's left arm. But he didn't stop moving as his forward momentum pushed him into Bodie's gun hand. He landed on the ground, while the weapon skittered off on the tarmac.

Rolling, he prepared himself to spring back up and put the madman down. Bodie was hovering over him and staring with raw hatred in his eyes.

Travis took a breath, ready to fight through the pain in his arm. Without a weapon and despite his wound, he could still easily take this guy out.

But in the next instant, what he saw made any more efforts unnecessary. As if out of nowhere, a row of bullet holes had suddenly appeared across Bodie's chest. The madman gawked down at them with a stunned look in his eyes. Glaring at Travis as if to say, "You lied," he never had a chance to open his mouth, before falling to his knees on the asphalt.

Then another bullet hole silently appeared in his forehead and Bodie quietly fell backward for the last time. Bodie Barnes would never have another word to say.

For a fleeting second Travis was furious at the sheriff. He'd had the guy. Another couple of minutes and Bodie would've been carted off to an institution, where he couldn't hurt anyone ever again. Travis had intended to force Bodie to tell him if someone had really been helping him, or if that had only been Bodie blowing hot air.

"Travis?" Summer's weak voice turned him in her direction, and he used his one good arm to drag himself to her side. "Is he gone?" she asked. "Are you all right?"

"Bodie's dead and I'm okay, sugar. Are you hurt?"

"The pain's finally going away. But I'm afraid I may have separated a shoulder." She leaned up on one elbow and watched him coming nearer. "You're *not* okay. You've been shot."

She lifted her head and started to shout. "Help! Somebody help us!"

Her voice was strong and clear, and he was relieved to hear her seemingly well enough to be yelling. So relieved that, when he looked down and saw a heavy stream of blood rolling down his useless left arm, his mind blanked. Then his vision blurred as he jumped off that high cliff of pain and fell right into a dark, black void.

Chapter 18

After only forty-eight hours, Summer was already frustrated with her injuries. But fortunately for her, the pain had become manageable with aspirin. Now she just wanted to see Travis and get out of the hospital.

"When are they discharging you?" The voice was similar to Travis's, but it belonged to his brother.

She looked up and saw Gage lounging against the threshold to her room. "The nurse tells me a doctor should sign my release papers this afternoon. Not a moment too soon. Have you seen Travis?"

Gage nodded. "Not for long, but he's out of ICU and can talk. He's asking for you."

Her free hand automatically went to her messy hair. "I'll have to ask the nurse to help me get dressed. Having my shoulder immobilized in this odd, uplifted position is annoying. But they tell me it won't be this way for long, and at least the two Taser barb injuries are feeling better and almost healed."

"What are your plans? Who'll help you when you're released?"

She'd been thinking over her plans since the night they'd been flown on the Bar-C's helicopter to this hospital, but talking to Travis came first. "I'm hoping to speak to Travis about that. Your aunt June has been here to see me and volunteered to let me stay with her until the shoulder is out of this sling. Jenna seems eager to help me out, too."

That thought made her smile. The seven-year-old hadn't been allowed in to see her yet. But Jenna had drawn get-well cards and sent wildflowers with June. Both of them wanted her to come home soon.

Sounded good. But in truth she really didn't have a home anywhere.

Travis would never send her away while she was still unable to fend for herself. She knew that. But what would happen when she was well?

"Talk to Travis." Gage smiled at her and gave her encouragement. "Will you continue searching for the guy you've been seeking? If so, I'll still help you."

"I'm not sure. He knows I'm here. He saw me. Maybe he's already left the area." Her quest to find Hoss was one of several things bothering her.

After the other night and all she and Travis had been through with Bodie, she was no longer positive as she had been about the importance of bringing her nemesis, Hoss, to justice. She felt changed and that confused her.

Gage shrugged. "Up to you. I'm sorry I was so hard on you before. But Travis had been hurt by someone he cared about in the past, and I didn't want to see that happen again."

"I know. And I also know Travis doesn't like liars. I've ruined his trust. I'm sorry for that, too."

Gage nodded and smiled again. "Glad to see you looking so well. Let me know if I can do anything to help you."

"Thanks." She tilted her head and thought of something else. "Oh, Gage. What happened with the bomb?"

"Sheriff McCord called in a bomb squad from San Antonio. They removed all the explosive materials from the cabin. But apparently Bodie didn't have enough knowledge to set things up properly. That C-4 is dangerous stuff, but the way it was handled would've never caused a real explosion."

"That's a relief. Thanks again."

Gage lifted his chin, winked at her and disappeared down the hall.

It was time. At last. She called for the nurse to help her get dressed. Ever since she and Travis had been brought into the hospital, she'd been getting bulletins from the nurses and June on his welfare. She'd been counting the minutes until she could see him for herself.

But now that the time was finally here, her insides began trembling as she worried about the future. Would this be one of the last times she ever saw Travis? Or would he forgive her so she could at least stay in Chance for Jenna's sake?

Still frustrated two hours later, after she'd finally managed to get dressed, Summer headed down the hall toward the elevator that would take her to Travis's room. She'd been going over and over what to say to him.

"Well, well. Look at you. All dressed and ready to go." Travis's aunt June stepped out of the elevator and beamed at her. "Good. Jenna is dying to see you."

"I'm going down to speak to Travis before we leave the hospital. He's been moved and wants to see me." The elevator doors closed and she pushed the button again.

"Yes, I know. I just stuck my head in his door, and he looks good. Shall I go pack your things while you talk to him?"

Summer stopped and sighed. "If you wouldn't mind. You've been so kind to me, June. I can't tell you how much I…"

"Nonsense," the older woman said with a wave. "You go on."

June started to turn, then turned back. "Oh. I almost forgot. Rosie and her fiancé are here. They want to speak to Travis after you do. I'm not sure, but I think she's going to tell Travis they'll put off the wedding until he's released so he can still stand up for Rosie."

"That's sweet of her."

"I thought so, too. They also said they needed to see you."

"Me? But why? I hardly know her and I don't know him at all."

June's eyes crinkled at the edges. "You've become very special to everyone. They're waiting down on Travis's floor in the alcove off the elevator. Ask them why for yourself."

"I will." The elevator door opened once again and she stepped inside. "I'll see you in a little while."

After the quick ride down two floors, Summer stepped from the elevator and looked for the alcove. Turning left, she headed around the corner.

And stopped dead in her tracks. The breath whooshed from her lungs and her knees started to shake.

There standing before her was the man she had been looking for and having nightmares about for the last five years. Bobby "Hoss" Packard. And Rosie, Travis's Rosie, was clinging to his arm as if she would die without him.

It couldn't be true. But it must be. Rosie's fiancé was the man who'd left her to die.

Speechless, Summer froze to the spot. She didn't know whether to scream or to run.

"Give R.J. a chance to talk to you," Rosie begged. "I know this is a big shock. It shocked me too when he told me this morning. But please hear him out. He's a good man who made a terrible mistake."

Summer found her voice and pinned Bobby or R.J. with a look that she hoped said she could start yelling for help at any time. "It took you long enough to come forward. If you're a 'good man,' I can't believe you would do this to someone as sweet as Rosie."

The man Rosie had called R.J. removed his cowboy hat and held it loosely in his hand. "You'd be right to think that, ma'am. But for so long I've been trying to tell myself that night never happened. That I was never there that day. I dunno. I guess I thought maybe if I stayed silent and worked hard, everyone back east would just forget about me."

She didn't know when she'd lost her fear of this man— maybe when he'd appeared with Rosie by his side. "Sorry to disappoint you. Were you hoping I hadn't survived that night? Or have you been hoping I wouldn't survive being kidnapped here?"

His face actually colored with embarrassment. "Neither one. I'm glad you survived—both times."

Something just occurred to her. "Who else have you told? Did Bodie Barnes know you were the one I've been searching for?"

"No, ma'am. No one else knows. Not yet. But I'm planning on going to the sheriff after we speak to Travis. I can't run anymore." He glanced down at Rosie beside him. "I honestly didn't think anyone would get hurt that night when we started out. And when I finally woke up and saw what my supposed boss meant to do, I tried to save you. I was the one who called 911. And I'll be eternally sorry that it was too little, too late."

It was true that someone else had called for help anonymously that night. But Summer remembered thinking it had been a passerby who hadn't wanted to become involved.

"Did you leave my ropes loose deliberately?"

He nodded but dropped his chin to stare at the floor. "But I couldn't get to the second floor without being seen. The guy I was with thought I'd seen too much of his mob connections and was waiting to kill me, along with the rest of you. But I've thought about you and your baby every day since then. It's time I paid for my stupidity. I'm only sorry that I came back to Chance and got Rosie involved."

"I'm not." Rosie spoke up. "I'm not sorry a bit. I believe you didn't mean to hurt anyone that night, and that you never knew the men who'd hired you were part of the mob." She took a breath that sounded more like a choked sob. "You were lost to me for so many years. Now that I've got you back, I'll never be sorry about what came before."

R.J. pleaded with his fiancée. "I love you. But you need to walk away. Now, before you're in too deep. I'm going to prison for a long time, sweetheart. Don't waste your life waiting for me."

"I'm good at waiting." Rosie crossed her arms over her chest with a determined look. "Already been waiting for you for most of my life. I'll still be there when you get out."

Summer's stomach clenched, understanding the pain these two were facing. "We need to talk this through some more. Let's go see Travis. He's good at knowing what to do."

"I thought so, too," Rosie agreed. Then she looked into Summer's eyes. "I know R.J. needs to turn himself in. If for no other reason than he can't live with what he's done. But if you said something about how he's changed and all, it might just help his case."

She would think about it. A lot. But at this moment, all Summer wanted to do was to see Travis. She'd never needed his strength more than she did right now.

Travis couldn't believe his eyes when he saw Summer. She looked pale and worried. And her injured shoulder was in a weird sling that was set at a funny angle and looked terribly uncomfortable. He'd been told she was healing and ready to leave the hospital. But she looked so weak and vulnerable; he didn't think she should even leave this room.

He'd wanted to be alone with her to talk about the two of them and where they went from here. And he couldn't wait to take her in his arms—make that, *arm.* His own shattered arm was in a cast and would stay that way for several weeks. They made quite a pair.

Instead of being able to talk by themselves, though, Rosie and her fiancé walked in behind Summer and stood beside his bed, waiting for a chance to spill their secret. He heard them out, but his eyes were glued to Summer the whole time. *Surprise* wouldn't quite describe the shock he felt at finding out that Summer's man was also Rosie's fiancé. But it was Summer who most concerned him.

When they were finished, he took Summer's hand in his. "How do you feel about all of this?"

"I'm not sure. I'd like to talk to you about it."

He shot a glare at R.J. "Summer's the one you owe the most. You ready to do whatever she feels is right?"

"Yes, sir. I wish it didn't have to hurt Rosie, but I'm willing to do whatever is necessary to face justice."

"Good. Then you and Rosie go on back to the Bar-C and wait there. Barrett will put you both to work for a couple of days until Summer can think things through."

"Thank you, Travis." Rosie leaned in to kiss his cheek. "I'm so glad to see you looking healthy. You'll be out of here in no time."

"Danged right." The doctors thought he needed another week. They didn't know Summer needed him more.

He turned once again to R.J. as he and Rosie started to leave. "You run again, and I'll hunt you down like a rabid coyote. You got that?"

"I won't run." R.J. settled his Stetson on his head and took Rosie's arm. "I owe you a lot for taking care of Rosie when I couldn't, Travis. I'm willing to pay you back any way I can. I'd do whatever you say."

Travis nodded but stayed silent until Rosie and R.J. left, then he turned to Summer and lifted his good arm to beckon her closer. "Come here." He felt hampered by having to stay in bed and decided he'd be up by this afternoon.

She sat at the edge of the bed, but that wasn't nearly close enough to suit him. "I'm so glad to see you," she said. "I've missed you. I haven't even thanked you for saving my life."

"Well, that just makes us even." He reached out to gently touch her right arm. "You saved my life, too. I was empty until you came along. Simply existing and getting by. When you arrived, you brought the sunshine back for both me and Jenna."

He felt the words dry up as water filled his eyes. And she was still too damned far away.

"Oh, Travis, I'm so sorry for lying to you about why I came to Chance." She looked down to where his hand lay against her arm. "I won't blame you for hating the lie, but please don't hate me forever. I couldn't stand it if you…"

"Hate you? Never. Hey, you've been around long enough to see that I've been known to tell a couple of big ones myself. Have you talked to Jimmy Stockard lately?"

She bit her lip, but the corners of her mouth crept up as though she was holding back a smile. "He told me what you said."

"See there? Nobody's perfect. We belong together."

Drawing a deep breath, she shook her head. "But… Gage thought I was being a terrible person. I didn't mean to lie to you or anyone. But that night has haunted me for so long. I…"

"Tell me," he offered softly. "Tell me all of it. I want to hear about the baby. Your husband. That night. All of it from your point of view."

At long last, she leaned into his good side and began to whisper. He held her, comforting her and letting her know that none of what happened had been her fault. It had suddenly become clear to him that she'd been blaming herself for her child's death all this time. Searching for the second man was just her way of dealing with guilt. And guilt was also the reason she'd believed the stalker had to be the man she'd been after.

But having her here beside him felt right. He just had to make her see that she was blameless in everything. And that he needed her.

She was crying softly by the time she finished, and he was surprised to find wetness on his own cheeks. They needed each other.

He leaned down and kissed her tears away. "It's done. Your child will be a part of you for as long as you live, and I will always love that part. But my child needs you, too. And so do I. You can be strong enough to live again with us, I know you can."

A low sound escaped her. "You still want me?" She looked at him with such intense desire that he would've liked to show her how much he wanted her right here.

Yes, he was going home from the hospital *tonight*.

"Want you?" He laughed instead of doing what he'd wanted. "Only *forever*. I love you. And you'll stay with me and marry Jenna and me because you love us, too."

"Pretty sure of yourself." She laughed too, and then kissed him so intensely that he didn't need to hear anything else.

This time it was for real. He would never wonder about love again. Real love and real life. He had it all. And he knew that together he and Summer and Jenna would surely find their happily ever after.

Epilogue

Two days later, on a sunny fall morning, Rosie stood outside the ranch house beside R.J. as the two of them said their I-do's. Summer found herself weeping just a little, knowing this was the last moment the couple would have together for a very long time.

She looked over at Travis, who was standing beside his daughter. He must've felt her looking and glanced her way with a nod. His sure strength ran through her and she straightened her spine. Everything seemed right.

After the ceremony, he made his way to her through the small crowd. "I sure hope a wedding was the right thing to do for Rosie."

"Of course it was," she assured him. "Just look at how happy she looks."

Rosie was beaming at her new husband.

"Well, it made Jenna happy to be in the wedding. And we'll all be glad to keep Rosie with us for a little while longer." Travis put his uninjured right arm around her waist. "Seeing as how the two of us aren't much good for anything, with these slings."

"Oh, I don't know about that." The image of the two of them in bed last night rippled a fresh desire through her veins. "You're still excellent at some things. Even with one arm pinned."

He chuckled and kissed her long and hard. She came up laughing and out of breath. "Remember where we are," she cautioned.

"I don't care. I don't care who sees how much in love we are. It'll be our turn for a wedding just as soon as we get back from Connecticut." He beamed at her as though they were the ones who'd just been married.

She loved this man with her whole being. "I've been meaning to thank you for all you're doing for R.J." Summer gazed into the eyes of the man she loved. "Without you talking to the state's attorney about R.J. testifying against the mob, and then hiring those high-powered lawyers for his defense, I'm sure he would've spent the rest of his life in prison."

"And you didn't want that." Not a question. They'd talked about it for hours on end, and she'd come to the decision that R.J. had reformed and, with Rosie's help, would never find himself in trouble again. Travis had approved and made it happen.

"R.J. will pay with his guilt for the rest of his days. But he can do some good in this world if he's outside of prison. I think he should get that chance."

She finally understood that she was meant to do some good in this world as well, and that giving to others would go a long way toward soothing her own guilt.

She had Travis to thank for showing her the way. And for so many more things.

He kissed her again. "Have I told you lately that I love you?"

"I never get tired of hearing it."

Never was a good word, in her book. That, along with Travis's favorite word, *forever,* applied to them from now on. No more disabling guilt. She had a wonderful new life and a family who loved her. And this time she knew the love would last forever.

* * * * *

SUSPENSE

COMING NEXT MONTH
AVAILABLE MAY 29, 2012

#1707 THE WIDOW'S PROTECTOR
Conard County: The Next Generation
Rachel Lee

#1708 MERCENARY'S PERFECT MISSION
Perfect, Wyoming
Carla Cassidy
A single mother and an ex-mercenary join forces to save her son and take down a cult leader.

#1709 SOLDIER'S PREGNANCY PROTOCOL
Black Ops Rescues
Beth Cornelison

#1710 SHEIK'S REVENGE
Sahara Kings
Loreth Anne White

REQUEST YOUR FREE BOOKS!
2 FREE NOVELS PLUS 2 FREE GIFTS!

◆ Harlequin®

ROMANTIC
SUSPENSE

Sparked by Danger, Fueled by Passion.

YES! Please send me 2 FREE Harlequin® Romantic Suspense novels and my 2 FREE gifts (gifts are worth about $10). After receiving them, if I don't wish to receive any more books, I can return the shipping statement marked "cancel." If I don't cancel, I will receive 4 brand-new novels every month and be billed just $4.49 per book in the U.S. or $5.24 per book in Canada. That's a saving of at least 14% off the cover price! It's quite a bargain! Shipping and handling is just 50¢ per book in the U.S. and 75¢ per book in Canada.* I understand that accepting the 2 free books and gifts places me under no obligation to buy anything. I can always return a shipment and cancel at any time. Even if I never buy another book, the two free books and gifts are mine to keep forever.

240/340 HDN FEFR

Name	(PLEASE PRINT)

Address	Apt. #

City	State/Prov.	Zip/Postal Code

Signature (if under 18, a parent or guardian must sign)

Mail to the **Reader Service:**
IN U.S.A.: P.O. Box 1867, Buffalo, NY 14240-1867
IN CANADA: P.O. Box 609, Fort Erie, Ontario L2A 5X3

Not valid for current subscribers to Harlequin Romantic Suspense books.

Want to try two free books from another line?
Call 1-800-873-8635 or visit www.ReaderService.com.

* Terms and prices subject to change without notice. Prices do not include applicable taxes. Sales tax applicable in N.Y. Canadian residents will be charged applicable taxes. Offer not valid in Quebec. This offer is limited to one order per household. All orders subject to credit approval. Credit or debit balances in a customer's account(s) may be offset by any other outstanding balance owed by or to the customer. Please allow 4 to 6 weeks for delivery. Offer available while quantities last.

Your Privacy—The Reader Service is committed to protecting your privacy. Our Privacy Policy is available online at www.ReaderService.com or upon request from the Reader Service.

We make a portion of our mailing list available to reputable third parties that offer products we believe may interest you. If you prefer that we not exchange your name with third parties, or if you wish to clarify or modify your communication preferences, please visit us at www.ReaderService.com/consumerschoice or write to us at Reader Service Preference Service, P.O. Box 9062, Buffalo, NY 14269. Include your complete name and address.

HRS11B

*Harlequin® Romantic Suspense presents the final book
in the gripping* PERFECT, WYOMING *miniseries
from best-loved veteran series author Carla Cassidy*

*Witness as mercenary Micah Grayson and cult escapee
Olivia Conner join forces to save a little boy and to take
down a monster, while desire explodes between them....*

Read on for an excerpt from
MERCENARY'S PERFECT MISSION

Available June 2012 from Harlequin® Romantic Suspense.

"**I** won't tell," she exclaimed fervently. "Please don't hurt me. I swear I won't tell anyone what I saw. Just let me have my other son and we'll go far away from here. I'll never speak your name again." Her voice cracked as she focused on his gun and he realized she believed he was Samuel.

Certainly it was dark enough that it would be easy for anyone to mistake him for his brother. When the brothers were together it was easy to see the subtle differences between them. Micah's face was slightly thinner, his features more chiseled than those of his brother.

At the moment Micah knew Samuel kept his hair cut neat and tidy, while Micah's long hair was tied back. He reached up and pulled the rawhide strip, allowing his hair to fall from its binding.

The woman gasped once again. "You aren't him...but you look like him. Who are you?" Her voice still held fear as she dropped the stick and protectively clutched the baby closer to her chest.

"Who are you?" he countered. He wasn't about to be taken in by a pale-haired angel with big green eyes in this evil place where angels probably couldn't exist.

HRSEXP0612

"I'm Olivia Conner, and this is my son Sam." Tears filled her eyes. "I have another son, but he's still in town. I couldn't get to him before I ran away. I've heard rumors that there was a safe house somewhere, but I've been in the woods for two days and I can't find it."

Micah was unmoved by her tears and by her story. He knew how devious his brother could be, and Micah would do everything possible to protect the location of the safe house. There was only one way to know for sure if she was one of Samuel's "devotees."

Will Olivia be able to get her son back from the clutches of evil? Or will Micah's maniacal twin put an end to them all? Find out in the shocking conclusion to the PERFECT, WYOMING *miniseries.*

MERCENARY'S PERFECT MISSION
Available June 2012, only from
Harlequin® Romantic Suspense, wherever books are sold.

SPECIAL EDITION

Life, Love and Family

USA TODAY bestselling author

Marie Ferrarella

enchants readers in

ONCE UPON A MATCHMAKER

Micah Muldare's aunt is worried that her nephew is going to wind up alone in his old age...but this matchmaking mama has just the thing! When Micah finds himself accused of theft, defense lawyer Tracy Ryan agrees to help him as a favor to his aunt, but soon finds herself drawn to more than just his case. Will Micah open up his heart and realize Tracy is his match?

Available June 2012

Saddle up with Harlequin® series books this summer and find a cowboy for every mood!

Available wherever books are sold.

www.Harlequin.com

HSE65674

Harlequin® *Romance*

A touching new duet from fan-favorite author

SUSAN MEIER

First Time **DADS!**

When millionaire CEO Max Montgomery spots
Kate Hunter-Montgomery—the wife he's never forgotten—
back in town with a daughter who looks just like him, he's
determined to win her back. But can this savvy business tycoon
convince Kate to trust him a second time with her heart?

Find out this June in

THE TYCOON'S SECRET DAUGHTER

And look for book 2 coming this August!

NANNY FOR THE MILLIONAIRE'S TWINS

Saddle up with Harlequin® series books this summer
and find a cowboy for every mood!

www.Harlequin.com